MW01101305

If You Knew Sally

By Rex Sicka

ISBN 978-0-692-01318-2

Library of Congress control number 2011902816

Introduction

    Any work of fiction contains elements of truth. This story, though fictitious in nature, is strongly founded upon the actual life of our title character. Sally Heiss is my Mother-In-Law. The entertaining and inspirational manner she has conducted her entire life is humbly presented in this volume as tribute. These pages contain few embellishments, though at certain junctures speculation was required to fill gaps of memory or to descriptively re-create scenes and events. My desire has been to clearly portray Sally's remarkable life in a respectful, honorable tone while remaining consistent with the actual trials, tribulations, tragedies, and triumphs of her life experience. I leave it to the reader's judgment.

Chapter 1

Maggie never wished death on her ex-husband but it was only his premature demise which would have her standing at his apartment door, key in hand. Zap O'Brien and she were four years divorced. In the intervening time she'd spoken to him but once. His death at only thirty one years of age was difficult to envision. Zap's attorney reaffirmed Maggie's recollection that Zap was not afflicted by any diseases or inherent weaknesses either could recall. His heart simply stopped beating in the total absence of symptoms or warning signs.

Maggie and Zap met over a decade earlier on the campus of NYU where they were enrolled; Zap a journalism major, Maggie undeclared. A torrid love affair developed lasting through graduation and culminating in a four year failed marriage. For a time, young love coursing through their veins made it seem as though it would last forever but the demanding realities of work a day living soon replaced youthful passions. The lack of a mutual vision doomed Maggie and Zap's union.

The years since their divorce reduced the frequency of instances when Zap invaded Maggie's thoughts which made this current situation difficult to grasp. His sudden death must have surprised even the victim because he had not executed a Will; the reason Zap's attorney contacted Maggie. The attorney, Vince, was another college acquaintance so he was familiar with the close friendship between Maggie, Zap, and Zevon, the other of their college threesome. During the final three years of their education they had been inseparable. Maggie was dutifully squandering her parent's investment in her education while Zap and Zevon were putting forth the absolute minimum effort pursuing journalism degrees with their respective parent's money. Zap chose journalism for the freedom he envisioned it would enable for him as a career choice. Zevon was a follower so any major would suffice. Zap once confided in Maggie he'd always written because it provided an excuse to be left alone, absent teachers and parents.

Zevon was supposed to meet Maggie at Zap's apartment. She'd hoped he would arrive on time this once. Not Zevon. Reluctantly, Maggie slid the key into the deadbolt. She took a deep breath before gently turning the key. She removed the key and held that breath as she turned the doorknob to open the door a crack. A warm gust of air brushed past her face causing Maggie to slightly recoil as if it were the spirit of Zap who'd escaped past her senses. Maggie regained her composure, pushing the door open far enough to peer into the darkness of Zap's apartment.

Maggie's eyes struggled to find focus in the dim light. She filled her lungs with the escaping scent as if she'd somehow sense his presence. Maggie was deeply conflicted about how she should feel regarding Zap's death and also about being inside his residence. There was a time when she was certain they'd be together forever. When they divorced she swore she never wanted to see him again. Never again would she waste her emotions on his uncaring self. Zap O'Brien, in Maggie's eyes, was incapable of sharing; his thoughts, time, pain, sorrow, but especially his love. How thoughtful he was now sharing his death. At the time of their divorce Maggie would have cheered his destruction but standing at his doorstep, memories and lost passions tugged at her heart.

Vince requested Maggie's presence to sort through Zaps' possessions, along with Zevon's assistance; because the window of opportunity would close quickly once the state was notified of his death coupled with his lack of a Last Will and Testament. Probate laws and courts existed for exactly this reason; the government wanted a cut. Maggie assured Vince any item of value would find its way to

Zap's parents or whomever else Vince designated. She and Zevon would transfer all materials of personal or sentimental value to the basement storage area of which Vince had provided a key. Their further charge was to ensure nothing would be found which would incriminate or embarrass Zap, not that he was a criminal but neither was he a choir boy.

Maggie was frozen in place at the doorway, unable to take the initial step into Zap's domain. What if she caught a faint whiff of his familiar scent? What if there were pictures hanging on the walls of she and Zap when they were still a couple? What if the apartment was littered with clues of a hedonistic or fetish lifestyle he'd hidden from her? What if the stench of death still fogged the air?

"Maggie May. Nice to see you." A familiar voice from the past snapped her from the immobile trance gripping her.

She turned to see Zevon's sheepish grin. She hadn't seen him in nearly four years but every contour of his face was familiar, instantly taking her back to the carefree days of their shared past. Maggie had met Zevon before she'd met Zap. It was Zevon who introduced the soon to be lovers. Seeing him was the breach releasing a flood of memories.

Tall, trim, and handsome Zevon; still wearing his trademark wireframe glasses atop the perfect, straight nose highlighting a classic, square jawed Midwestern face. His hair was jet black, lacking the slightest hint of gray but, as she remembered, meticulously styled for the illusion he actually cared little about his cultured, unkempt hairstyle. Zevon's physique was aerobics class trim. The girls always spotted Zevon first. When they'd met, Maggie and Zevon discovered quickly they could be good friends but romantic entanglements would never work. He was not Maggie's type. She could see through the slick charm he employed to disrobe unsuspecting coeds but Maggie and Zevon were perfect verbal foils for one another; spirited banter bounced between them as if they were reading from a rehearsed script. Verbal gymnastics began the moment they met, not ending until the day Zevon left New York for Chicago. Zevon was the other half of 'ZZ over-the-top', he and Zap's two member party fraternity, and with the addition of Maggie they were the three inseparable amigos. Together they cracked sarcastic from their self-appointed hilltop about the hapless minions wandering aimlessly around campus. They knew the answers the others sought in vain. Life lay stripped bare before their judging eyes. There were neither mysteries nor surprises for the three enlightened youths.

"Pretty boy. Sorry to see you again, especially like this." Maggie embraced her old friend.

Neither hurried to release the hug, knowing upon release they'd be required to speak of Zap's sudden death and neither possessed the words. The three amigos were too young to be wrestling with the concept of mortality.

Zevon released first, stepping back to take in the full length of his long lost friend. His soft brown eyes, which had seduced a hundred girls, surveyed the length of Maggie's svelte figure. "I don't know what to say, Mags. I haven't had a clue since Vince called yesterday. As much as I wanted to see you, I knew I wouldn't know what to say. This came out of nowhere." The smile faded and his brown eyes drifted to the floor.

Maggie saw the pain ingrained into Zevon's face. She asked, "Has he been ill?"

He enthusiastically replied, "No, nothing. That's why it doesn't make any sense. We just went out on the town Wednesday night. I talked to him yesterday morning. He stayed home from the paper to finish an article. He was going to fax it to me by three o'clock. When the fax didn't show, I called, but no one answered. I knew something was up. Zap might blow off a lot of things but never a deadline. I called his Super. He's the one who found him. Zap's heart just quit. No one knew he even had heart issues. I don't think Zap new. He never said anything to me. Did you know?"

Maggie was clueless, also. "No. He didn't like to exercise but he wasn't in bad shape the last time I saw him. He drank but I never saw him smoke."

Zevon stepped forward. "Let's go inside. We probably shouldn't stand in the hall. Some of his neighbors likely saw the coroner pack him out."

He groped the wall for the light switch he knew was there from many previous visits. Zevon flipped the switch and light flooded onto the worldly possessions of Zap's private universe. Zevon, having been in the apartment, quickly scanned the room to see if anything looked out of place. His clinical brain was still searching for a different nefarious reason for Zap's death other than a heart attack.

Maggie had never seen Zap's residence. She searched for hints of the man with which she once shared space. She pried for clues into the evolution of the man since their separation. The living room was neat and sparsely furnished. An overstuffed leather couch faced a sixty inch flat screen television hanging on the wall. The only other furniture was a mass produced, segmented computer workstation with a gray fabric, castered chair placed in front. The desk was devoid of clutter. The flashing light on the keypad denoted the unit was turned on but the flat screen LCD monitor was dark. The only wall decorations were framed movie posters; 'The African Queen', 'The Maltese Falcon', 'Annie Hall',' Midnight Cowboy', and 'Attack of the Fifty Foot Woman'.

The kitchen could be viewed through an open breakfast bar and, like the rest of the apartment, was sparse and neat. A garage sale table complete with two yellow vinyl chairs and a coffee maker were the only things visible except for a wooden wine rack, stocked with a dozen bottles of wine.

Maggie looked at everything and nothing. "What are we supposed to be looking for? This is too strange. I don't even know how to feel. I spent the last four years trying to get him out of my head and now here I am again. I don't understand why I need to be here. Why would Vince call me? How did he even get my phone number? I don't have anything to do with Zap's life anymore. We didn't speak and I didn't leave anything behind."

11

Zevon was perplexed. "Don't ask me. Vince was here when they took Zap out and he said you and me should be here. You may have called it quits but you're still the only woman who has ever meant anything to him."

Maggie recognized the soft voice from Zevon. "Don't patronize me with your bimbo voice, Z. Zap used the same crap on me. When he let up for a time, I thought it was because of me. I really believed we had a chance but all he did was switch tactics. He didn't have room for me. He didn't have room for anyone. I just wasn't smart enough to see it, for a while."

Zevon pocketed his charm. "You're right. Zap was self-centered and a loner at heart but don't short change yourself. What he felt for you was real, Mags. Remember, it was me who was here after you left him. He was hurt. I've been around for every relationship Zap had since junior high and I'm here to tell you, no woman has ever gotten to him like you did. Vince called you because of something Zap said one night when the three of us were out on the town. It couldn't have been more than a few weeks ago. It was one of those sappy 'I love you, man' kinds of drunks. Well, Zap let a little of his private self slip out. He told Vince if anything ever happened to him, he should contact you. Zap wanted you to have his belongings, especially

12

the things you two obtained together. Zap said at the very least, you should have the option to throw it all away." Zevon grinned. "Don't you think about those days? I do, all the time. The three of us were the best times I've ever had. When I was growing up in Dayton, I was scared to death about finding my way in the world. Everybody seemed to be more capable and better prepared than me. Zap showed me how to laugh at everyone and everything. It was like he figured out life early on and the rest of us didn't get it. I just wanted to be part of it. I know you felt it, too."

Maggie's upper lip curled into a sneer. "Oh, I felt it alright. It's called contempt and indifference. Zap didn't have any answers; he just figured if the world was going to bitch slap you anyway, you might as well slap them back first. What I saw was a man with more potential than anyone I've ever met and he was hell bent on squandering it. Zap wasn't happy and I couldn't make him happy. I got tired of watching and I didn't want to go down in flames beside him." Maggie's entire body stiffened. "Tell you what, Z. Why don't you go through his things? If you come across something you think I might want, send it to me. Better yet, burn it."

Without a response to Maggie's bitter statement, Zevon turned around to move the computer mouse so he could see what was on Zap's monitor. A page of text appeared but it was an envelope, partially hidden under the keyboard, which caught his attention. He picked the envelope up from the desk. "Mags, it's addressed to you. It's stamped and ready to mail."

Maggie accepted the envelope. Taking a seat on the sofa, she tore it open and removed a single sheet of paper;

Dearest Maggie,

I hope this letter finds all well in your life. I am writing this final time because I must share a life changing event. But first, allow me to apologize for all the unfairness I heaped upon you. You reached out to me but I was too proud, too stupid, and too misdirected to accept your hand. I didn't understand. Though our paths will likely never cross again, I wanted you to know something extraordinary has happened. I met someone who pulled back the curtain which has shielded my eyes these many years. She lifted the veil obscuring life. Everything was before me all along; free will, choice, you. Never again will I bemoan my fate. I will look only forward.

I'm going to make it, Maggie. You're the only person to whom I needed to say

14

those words. I know you'll understand. I would not have survived without you.

Hugs, Superstar.

My love, Zap

His words grabbed hold of her emotions before she could prepare a defense for the tidal wave of memory washing over her. The tears streamed down her unprepared cheeks as she silently held out the letter to Zevon's curious hand.

Zevon read Zap's letter, carefully folded it, and handed it back to Maggie. Her tear stained face looked expectantly, searching for Zevon's reaction. Softly he said, "Talk about bad luck. Zap finally sees the light and then he's gone."

Maggie had to know. "Who's the woman, Z? One of the typical bimbae? It doesn't sound like it."

"I haven't got a clue. As far as I knew he wasn't seeing anyone. When he went out it was usually with me." Zevon spun on the computer chair and began scrolling to the beginning of the text on Zap's computer. "The only thing out of the ordinary is he's made several trips to Arizona. He was researching something but he hadn't shared with me what he was working on. Other than that it's been business as usual."

"You're his editor. Why wouldn't he tell you what he's researching?" Maggie asked.

Zevon shrugged, "You know Zap. He didn't like anyone to see anything but a finished product. Originally he went to Arizona for an article about this old World War Two pilot who rebuilt a P – 58 Mustang fighter plane in his backyard. Zap turned in the story but he kept going back to Arizona. Personally, I hoped he'd found something that inspired him to begin writing his novel. Zap really was a great writer. I used to tell him it would be a travesty if he never wrote a novel." Zevon was at the beginning of the text. "Check this out, Mags. Maybe this is the mystery woman. It's a manuscript titled 'If You Knew Sally'."

Maggie peered over his shoulder. "Read it, Z. I'd love to know what kind of woman could spin his cynical head."

Chapter Two

Call it destiny, call it determination, but there are consequential events which occur by sheer force of will. The force is not driven by strength, thoughtful reflection, or conscious decisiveness. The event arrives without fanfare, trumpets, or even a forgettable sigh. The event is life and it arrives with or without our consent. Life requires but one interaction and that action is a form of choice, though life's choice is elegantly simple; accept or reject. There are neither covenants nor conditions. There are no bargains for negotiation. Life simply is life.

There are many incarnations associated with the majesty of life. Daily these processes happen and cannot be denied. Many begin surrounded by great hope while others arise through acts of great violence.

The year was 1928 and optimism and hope flowed seamlessly to every corner of America. The war to end all wars was over, propelling the country to new heights; politically, economically, and militarily. America was officially a superpower. The sky was the limit and every citizen was infected by the dynamic new energy.

Three centuries of colonialist expansion suddenly gave way to the imperialism of the 20th century. Geographical lines were drawn and numerous new countries were created by the dictates of war. All that remained was the allocation of the resources.

Wall Street, empowered by the creation of the privately owned Federal Reserve System fifteen years earlier, was riding a financial high with seemingly unlimited possibility. Wealth seemed within the reach of any bold enough to pursue their fortune. The roaring twenties roared from the economic boom spawned of new financial inventions from the minds of America's greatest moneychangers. The explosion reached the farthest corners of the vast country.

Those corners were now accessible as the world became smaller. Air travel opened avenues long unthought about as destinations. Charles Lindbergh connected the two great continents of power. Henry Ford's automated assembly lines built affordable automobiles offering freedom of movement before unknown to the general public.

In the Northern California town of Santa Rosa, eighty miles north of San Francisco, Madeline Astor Baber was offered a ride home from a gathering of young friends by the brother of her friend, Marion Green. Madeline lived in Santa Rosa, a city alive with possibility much like the rest of the country.

She was also in the front row of a generation empowered with freedoms never before enjoyed by the sisterhood of women anywhere in civilized society. Women could vote, drive, and even dance with wild abandon.

Spring was in the air in Madeline's coastal world and the opportunity to ride in an automobile where she could see and be seen was irresistible. In 1928, the opportunity to breeze down the coastal highway where peers could witness her personal freedom was one of the pinnacle events of being a young woman of her time.

The ride in Harold's Model A was the thrill Madeline believed it would be right up until the time he turned off of the main road. She was to bear violent witness to a reality known to women since time memorial. There are ruthless men whose twisted compulsions deny respect for the sanctity of the female body. Madeline Baber was raped by someone she trusted. The event transpired in broad daylight.

The court of public opinion cares little if the time is the roaring twenties, the permissive sixties, or the medieval dark ages; an unmarried, pregnant woman was an embarrassment and an abomination. Since the advent of original sin, rape victims are always looked upon as somehow responsible for their predicament as if sexual violence cannot occur without enticements from the victim. Laws written to protect male dominance and property leave women with little choice but to be victims once again should they pursue justice from their attackers.

Neither hope nor prayer could prevent a fetus from growing in Madeline's womb. Her choices were limited and extremely daunting. Clinical, antiseptic abortion was available only for the wealthy elite. Black market abortion in working class America was conducted in back alley rooms with unsterilized instruments by men with questionable medical backgrounds. Carrying a baby to term and raising the child would place a cloud of stigma Madeline could never escape.

Madeline and her humiliated mother reached the only decision which made sense. When Madeline's condition could no longer be concealed from prying eyes, she and Mom would temporarily relocate to San Francisco where the ill-gotten baby would be born and placed up for adoption.

Their plan was executed and the fateful day arrived. Madeline's hospital room was a bevy of activity after she successfully gave birth to a healthy baby girl. A nurse removed the prospective adoptee at once to prevent bonding between mother and child, leaving Madeline, her humiliated mother, another nurse, and a representative from the adoption agency.

The quick removal of the newborn stirred conflicting emotions within young Madeline. She'd avoided being labeled a harlot in the community where she lived but it would never console the guilt she would carry to her grave. Society and youth view the world through short-term lenses but, as Madeleine was to discover, giving up your flesh and blood is a gift of pain that keeps on giving. There were no guidance counselors or self-help books to direct her through this trying ordeal. The violent act which created this child would linger, surfacing in Madeline's nightmares throughout her life but the act of abandoning the baby which resulted would haunt her forever. No matter the moral battles, Madeline still had to survive the day's process.

The duty nurse checked Madeline's vital signs while Mom and an impatient hospital administrator waited his turn to question the young mother. The woman representing the adoption service stood silently in the doorway. The administrator and the adoption service needed a name for the birth certificate.

Neither Madeline nor her mother had given any thought of a name for a baby they would never see again. Both, naturally, believed the adoption agency or the adoptive parents would name the child. Panic ensued as the hospital administrator pressed Madeline for a name to complete the paperwork.

Madeline offered up the name Betty, a name she favored for reasons she didn't offer, but the official needed also a last name. Madeline and her mother agreed they didn't want their last name or the name of the father to appear on the baby's birth certificate. Madeline's name might require explanation at some later date and she wanted to provide her newborn with one gift; never to know of her predator father.

The administrator explained, with disdain, the slot assigned for the birth father would be filled with 'Illegitimate' if Madeline didn't provide a name. Illegitimate would be a scarlet letter the young girl would bear throughout her entire life. Society loves to perpetuate their collective judgments. Still the baby required a full name. The officials impatience was obvious, he making no effort to conceal disgust for the, obviously, promiscuous young girl.

Madeline frantically searched the faces surrounding her for a clue. None were

22

forthcoming. The nurse conducted her duties indifferent to the girl's dilemma. Mom avoided eye contact with everyone she encountered. The administrator's judging eye bore heavily into the new mother. The adoption worker remained in the doorway offering no sign of help. From Madeline's hospital bed a wall sign could be seen, though partially obscured, over the shoulder of the woman in the doorway.

Madeline blurted out the baby's last name for the official birth record; King. The adoption worker stepped into the room to record the baby girl's name on her paperwork revealing the entire sign hanging on the pale green walls of the hospital hallway. Betty Jean King was officially named after the last four letters of a 'no smoking' sign.

The frantic beginning of Betty Jean King's official life became even more confused when somehow the adoption papers listed her as Sara. No matter, once the adoption was completed the world would know her as Sally except in private moments with her adoptive father who lovingly referred to his daughter as Butch.

So it began. Sally was adopted by a loving couple from Raymond, Washington. The couple, William and Margarite Christie, already had a four-year-old daughter but sadly, could not conceive another. Margarite, driven by the news of her sister's newest pregnancy, implored Bill, as William was known, to provide her with a second child. Bill agreed without dissent.

Bill informed the adoption agency of his desire for a blonde haired, blue-eyed baby boy and, in the efficiency of bureaucracy; they provided Bill and Margarite with a brunette, brown eyed baby girl. How could they resist?

Sally Christie would live, love, and prosper on the shores of Willapa Bay among mountains of oyster shells, in the shadow of rain forests. Sally didn't fuss, seldom did she cry, and she possessed an unquenchable smile that melted the hearts of all who met her. The Christie's new daughter was alert, inquisitive, and full of life.

Honeymoons, no matter how endearing or memorable, always come to an end and at the tender age of one, baby Sally was diagnosed with the scourge of the age, dreaded polio. In 1929, being afflicted with polio offered few options; the life of a cripple or death. The life-saving vaccine developed by Dr. Jonas Salk was still many years in the future. Doctors offered little hope to Bill and Margarite for their daughter. The medical community shared only condolences.

Margarite shared the tragic news with a neighbor while hanging the family's clothes on the line behind their house. As luck would have it, her neighbors were chiropractors which educated them in the art of alternative therapies. They offered to try a new technique for treating Sally's affliction. Though the Christie's barely knew their neighbors, in the absence of alternatives, they agreed to allow the two chiropractors to treat little Sally.

The methodology was straightforward; for twenty four grueling hours, tiny Sally was subjected to the application of hot and cold compresses in concert with continuous massage. Bill joined with his ultra-religious wife in prayer for their daughter. It couldn't hurt.

Their efforts were rewarded, the prayers answered, though baby Sally never appeared to foster a doubt. She didn't complain nor resist, emerging with a smile on her face, a trait she never relinquished. Little Sally would go forth with club feet, weak legs, and an uncanny ability to ignore the taunts and stigmas normally attached to a cripple. Sally never accepted the cripple tag. She gleefully embraced her life devoid of questions and with a steadfast refusal to allow limitations in her life.

Unconditional acceptance is empowerment. Acceptance declares your life your own. Barriers to the empowered are simply obstacles to be overcome. Even as an infant, Sally refused to be denied. Her first breath was her own and she refused to relinquish dominion of her life to anyone. Somewhere within her spirit she granted herself license to live the life she imagined. Her gaze would be forever forward and she would march with a smile and a song. Defiance would greet parents, teachers, doctors, or any who dared suggest there was something she could not accomplish; leg braces and crutches be damned.

The Christie family relocated to the western shore of Willapa Bay, in the small town of Nahcotta on the Long Beach Peninsula, when Sally was four years old. The peninsula is a twenty five mile long sand spit originating at the northern banks of the Columbia River. After moves from two rental houses they settled into a two story house with a backyard adjoining the tide flats of Willapa Bay. Sally and her older sister were home. Nahcotta was twelve miles north, on a gravel road, of the bustling seaside town of Long Beach.

Their house was built on piers so as not to be washed away during extreme tides. The outhouse would flood during spring neap tides making the thoughtful act of trudging to the facility at night, forsaking the usual indoor pot, a pointless endeavor as feces floated around their feet.

The peninsula would become Sally's playground. When the cow was milked and properly staked, the chickens fed and eggs collected, and all other chores completed; Sally was free to explore her world. Whether jumping off the garage with an umbrella in hand to see if she could fly, donating another pair of shoes to the depths of mud on the beach, or rowing raccoons to the safety of Long Island behind their house; this was Sally's world. Her sister, Mary Jane, known to all as Chris in her youth, was raised by the very same parents under the very same roof but they couldn't be more different. Chris strived to please everyone while Sally sought only her own approval. Chris was a doting daughter, a dutiful student, and a consonant parishioner. Sally marched to a guiding tune only she could hear. Something simmered deep within which drove her on no matter what path she chose. Somehow, somewhere Sally always knew she was different. Chris would never defy authority while Sally wore defiance as a badge of courage. Though, four years junior, it was always Sally who stood steadfast in defense of Chris and herself.

Sally was the sparkle in her father's eye and the pain in her mother's butt. Margarite was a teetotaler and a devoted Presbyterian who never accepted the evil of demon alcohol or relented in her disdain for anyone not present at church services. Bill and Marguerite engaged in verbal battle many nights while Sally and Chris eavesdropped; the battle always over his penchant for drink. Margarite loved her family but her love was filtered through a thick veneer of self-righteousness. She spent all of her life attempting to mold her family into the perfect picture of purity which she wanted the outside world to see. Her vision was her obsession and she raved, manipulated, and cajoled her husband and her daughters to conform to her will. Margarite's nagging ways inspired her husband to seek employment opportunities which would keep him away for weeks and months at a time.

Bill's long absences affected Chris little but Sally missed her father. He understood his headstrong adoptive daughter while Marguerite would never understand her. Bill Christie was a loving man with a heart of gold, especially when it came to Butch, his blonde haired, blue-eyed boy.

Sally was enrolled in school at the age of four not because of her age but because she was unusually large for her age. The one-room schoolhouse in Nahcotta was run by

Ms. Nagle, a visual throwback to another century. She wore floor length dresses, button-down shoes, and a bun tying her hair so tightly behind her head, her stern eyes struggled to blink. Ms. Nagle taught boys and girls up to the eighth grade. Her teaching technique required strict adherence to discipline. Sally would prove to be a challenge.

Schoolyard life and student activities were an exciting new adventure for young Sally. She was free of Mother's scorn, only to be confronted with Ms. Nagle's strict justice. School was also Sally's first experience with the cruelty of peer pressure. Cripples with leg braces are quickly singled out for the most intense taunting and teasing. Most handicapped children retreat to inner sanctums under the relentless onslaught. Sally reacted differently since she didn't recognize her affliction as a handicap. Sally noticed quickly, with her crutches, she was the only one in the schoolyard with a weapon. Why should she be defensive when she was the only one armed for offense? Many years after sharing the schoolyard with Sally, classmates would commiserate scars they'd received at the hands of poor little crippled Sally. A rebel was born.

Ink wells in the school's classroom would mysteriously be filled with tadpoles. Fragrant bouquets of skunk cabbage appeared on Ms. Nagle's desk as if by magic. Scaling the bell tower was off limits to students but was child's play for Sally. Invariably the hanging rope for ringing the school bell would be left hung out of Ms. Nagle's reach. It was Sally's world and all the other inhabitants needed to get used to the idea.

Sally began developing a mantra she would carry as a rallying cry throughout the length of her life; 'Don't let the bastards get you down'. Truer words were never spoken.

The one-room schoolhouse burned to the ground after Sally's first year. It wasn't by her hand but certainly with her blessing. The new school was 1930's state-of-the-art; indoor plumbing, gymnasium, four classrooms, even a cafeteria where the children were served spanish rice, Jell-O, and cornbread. Hot lunches were a glorious bonus as the country slid into depression.

Ms. Nagle gladly promoted Sally into the care of Mrs. Moore and the second grade. The second grade was also the official beginning of Sally's war against authority. Her second year of school she reached another milestone; the beginning of seven years of lengthy stays at the Shriners Hospital in Portland, Oregon for treatment of her polio.

There are people who possess a talent for capturing a moment in time. Sometimes in a story, a photograph, or a painting they'll trap a mood or a spirit. Norman Rockwell is a master of doing just such a thing in his works portraying American daily life. One such painting is of a young girl seated on a faded, wooden bench outside the principal's office. One tail of a white button-down shirt hangs loosely over a wrinkled, plaid, quilted skirt. White mud stained socks lay rumpled atop scuffed, untied saddle shoes. Her hair is tied into ruffled pigtails bursting free one strand of hair at a time. Red ribbons cling hopelessly to her braids. A bandage covers an injury on one knee while the other proudly displays its abrasion. A dark circle underlines one eye, the remnant of another day's battle. A missing tooth complements her shiner as testament to her fighting spirit. The girl's disheveled appearance paints the background but it's her unrepentant smile which tells her tale.

Mr. Rockwell, undoubtedly, painted this particular scene as a re-creation of a vision from his past or his own schoolyard experiences. Little did he realize when he sat down to create his insight, the finished masterpiece was a snapshot of Sally Christie's school years.

Sally presented a dilemma for teachers and administrators. They couldn't take the crutches away from the handicapped girl but leaving them in her possession meant pain for any classmate bold enough to tease her. The solution was to keep promoting her from grade to grade and soon she would be the problem of Illwaco High School. The tactic made perfect sense due in large part to Sally's unusual size for her age. If they were to hold her back one grade level, not only would they have to deal with her another year but her tormentor's beatings would surely increase in severity as she grew.

No matter due to sympathy or self-preservation, Sally continued to be promoted taking her consistent 'F' grade average with her to the next level.

Sally's stays at the Shriners Hospital were welcome temporary respites from Mother and teachers as well as for Mother and teachers. Most of the children at the hospital were terrified to be away from the comfort and safety of home. Sally saw only another adventure. Bill Christie was working as an engineer on the construction of the Bonneville Dam on the Columbia River during the time Sally was at the hospital. The massive project was part of President Franklin Delano Roosevelt's WPA projects putting America back to work during The Great Depression. The workers of America needed the boost of employment and the country needed the electrical power for growth.

Sally faced polio treatments without fear in large part because she knew she would never be alone. Her father wrote his infirmed daughter every day as well as visiting whenever his schedule would allow. Sally viewed her time away from her mother as private time for her and Dad. Sally would regale to the other children, doctors, and nurses stories of her father's importance to the Bonneville Dam project.

All the Northwest was abuzz as the completion of the dam neared. The lavish grand opening ceremony was planned and media pundits wrote of nothing else. Bonneville was on the lips of everyone. FDR, himself, was making the long trip west for the festivities. The eyes of the nation were on Bonneville. Sally was receiving treatment at the time of the grand opening. To her delight she was scheduled to attend the ceremony with a small delegation from the Shriners. Her father's involvement in the Bonneville project was partially responsible for Sally's selection but also a delightful wheelchair bound child, with polio like the President, was a perfect salutation to the leader of the free world.

With the exception of the players, politics change little with time. Issues relate to the currents of the country but tactics and public perceptions are much the same regardless of the time in history. The years of the Great Depression were some of the most tumultuous and trying political periods in American history. Whoever resides in the Oval Office during great turmoil will bear the brunt of public anger. FDR was no exception. History is much kinder to FDR than the citizens who lived through the hardest economic period in American history. Our president did not evoke middle of the road emotions; people either loved or hated him.

Bill Christie was a loyal Republican. He was not hired to work on the Bonneville Dam because of his politics. Bill was hired for his ability as an electrical engineer. Bill despised FDR and his liberal policies, though he understood the benefit of projects such as Bonneville, politically he viewed the president as a closet Socialist. Conservative media called FDR 'The Great Destroyer' and Bill readily agreed. The economy was faltering and most conservatives, Bill included, blamed the President. The Christie family sat through many lengthy tirades about how FDR was destroying America.

Politics aside, the joyous day of dedication for the Bonneville Dam and Power Generation Plant arrived. Banners flapped in the breeze. A brass band from Corvallis,

Oregon entertained the overflow crowd. Officials, elected and appointed, back slapped and glad handed one another as speaker after speaker sang praises to the President, the country, and the engineering feat before them.

Sally was seated in a wheelchair at the front of the crowd when FDR was wheeled to the podium. Her father stood behind her. It was a time of immense pride for the young girl as well as the country. The President's words floated above the crowd and across the waters of the mighty Columbia River. Neither his words nor the day would live in infamy but still he was dynamic and brief. Upon conclusion the crowd rose with thundering applause. The ceremony was coming to an end.

FDR's staff had already pinpointed the perfect photo opportunity to grace the front page of newspapers from New York to Los Angeles. What better than to have the polio stricken leader of the free world photographed shaking hands with a cherub cheeked child bound in a wheelchair by the very same disease? The newswires would eat it up.

FDR's people, followed by dozens of photographers, watched the President's wife, Eleanor, push her husband to face the smiling young polio victim. The scene would warm the hearts of ailing America. Franklin Delano Roosevelt saw a kindred spirit. The young girl saw only what she knew, The Great Destroyer. On a beautiful spring day before thousands of adoring fans, Sally Christie spit on the President of the United States.

Chapter 3

Maggie pushed away from the computer desk. "Great story, but who the hell is she? You mean he's never mentioned her?"

Zevon shook his head. "I haven't got a clue but I'd be willing to bet Sally is Zap's Arizona research project."

Maggie replied, "Well, if she was born in 1928 she's in her eighties now so I don't think it's a romantic involvement unless his tastes in women have changed dramatically."

His eyes were still glued to the monitor. "I don't think so. If anything he was going for younger women. He said they were easier to get naked and all the women our age had ticking biological clocks."

Maggie stood. "You want a drink? I need a drink." She didn't wait for an answer, walking into the kitchen to open a bottle of wine.

Zevon followed, leaning on the bar while Maggie poured two glasses. They sipped the Chablis as their eyes lazily wandered around the sparsely appointed apartment.

Maggie's attention found a way back to Zevon. "Why would Zap want to write to me; we were yesterday? Why wouldn't he write to his parents or to you? Why not tell you he had an epiphany?"

Zevon grinned. "Like it or not, Mags, you're the only person Zap ever loved and that includes his parents."

She scoffed. "Get real. Zap never loved anything or anyone in his whole, self-centered life. I was nothing but a safe place to hide while he figured out why the world was so screwed up. Zap wasn't capable of love. All he knew was contempt, sprinkled with a large dose of horny."

"You're wrong. It might not fit your definition of love but it was real to Zap. Every time he'd get sentimental drunk, he always talked about you, Mags. Like it or not you were the highs and the lows of his life." Zevon took a healthy pull on his wineglass. He didn't want to reveal too much of his best friend's inner recesses. He changed the subject. "Vince said Zap didn't want his parents notified if something happened to him. Zap told him to box up everything you didn't want and send it to them. That's it; no phone call, nothing. I don't know where they moved nor even if they're still alive, do you?"

Maggie shrugged, "No. All I know about his parents is they lied to him all his life. I don't think he ever forgave them. It was pretty strange to keep his roots a secret from him, I mean, did they really think he wouldn't notice he was a dark skinned Hispanic and his dad was a pasty white Irish guy. At some point they needed to fess up. It was bad enough they named him after Frank Zappa and then denied they were drug inspired hippies. They had to know Zap was smart enough to figure out they turned their backs on the past and everyone they knew. Just because they pretended their past didn't exist doesn't mean it didn't happen. Why would he respect them? They didn't respect him enough to tell him the truth. They lived a fairytale and got pissed if Zap questioned it."

Zevon was attentive. "Zap never talked much about his parents to me. Even in high school, he just shined them on. I never even thought about who his father might be. That's messed up." He drained his wine glass and refilled it. A wicked smile grew on his tailored face. "Maybe you and I should have hooked up. I could've saved you some pain."

Maggie chuckled. "You would have only given me a different kind of pain. You couldn't stay faithful to one woman if she chained you in her basement. The only reason we both wouldn't be here today is I would have already killed your sorry ass."

His grin grew in sheepish submission. "You're probably right. You're too smart for me anyway. I like a woman with long legs, big tits, and just smart enough to dress herself but not smart enough to stop me from undressing her. I definitely don't want her smart enough to find her way back to my apartment without an invitation."

All Maggie could do was smile in total agreement. Truer words were never spoken. "Now there's the Zevon I remember." She motioned to the computer. "What about this Sally woman? What is she all about? How could an old woman get to Zap? I didn't think anyone was capable of finding a weakness in his armor."

Zevon shrugged. "I don't know but, then again, I don't know who else it might be. I'm sure he wasn't seeing anyone here. Something changed. Since Zap went to Arizona for the story on that old pilot, his writing changed. There was real passion and emotion instead of his usual sarcastic, biting humor. Like I said, my hope was he was inspired by someone or something to finally start writing for himself. That's why I never questioned all the trips to Arizona. You don't mess with literary genius and Zap really was special. He could pull out a great article from the dark recesses us mere mortals didn't realize were there. What's strange to me is this

Sally story reads like a biography. That wasn't Zap's style. He pried around in the dark side of people."

A sudden thought sparked Maggie. "Wait a minute. We are assuming Sally is an actual person. What if she's a character he was creating? Zap never believed there were any answers or revelations in the world. It would make more sense if his enlightenment came from his own imagination."

Zevon couldn't quite accept Maggie's idea. "Maybe, but if Sally wasn't real why did he have to keep going to Arizona?"

"What if Sally is real but deceased and this story is a eulogy about someone he heard about in Arizona?" Asked Maggie.

Zevon pulled out his cell phone. "That's easy enough to check. The paper has the best researchers on the planet." He pressed a programmed number. "Gladys, this is Zevon. Would you check a birth record for me? It's from 1928 in San Francisco. The birth mother was Madeline Baber; the father was listed as George King. I'll wait."

Maggie's gaze drifted around the sparsely appointed room while Zevon waited for a response. The answer came quickly.

"Yes, I'm here," he said. Zevon nodded before saying, "Thanks, Gladys. You are the best." He closed the phone. "She's real, born December 15, 1928, at San Francisco General, a baby girl."

Maggie raised her glass, "Let's read some more."

Chapter 4

War defines countries as well as the generation whose members step forward to defend her. World War Two was the epitome of a citizenry rising as one for a singular purpose. No corner of America escaped the rigors or avoided their patriotic duty.

Long Beach was the front lines of a possible attack. The peninsula was exposed to the vast Pacific Ocean where a ruthless enemy lurked somewhere just beyond the horizon. In the minds and imaginations of the local residents, Japanese submarines patrolled below the waves awaiting their opportunity to attack. The threat was quite real. Fishing fleets from California to Alaska were enlisted to patrol the western shore of the country in search of Japanese warships. Artillery installations were installed in concrete reinforced bunkers looking out at the waters from every cliff top offering a clear vantage.

History textbooks tell students the war never reached the shores of America but those who lived on the Long Beach Peninsula and on the Oregon shore of the Columbia River knew better. Fort Stevens, west of Astoria, on two separate occasions experienced enemy shelling. Only a lack of casualties allowed government officials to deny the events.

Twenty five miles of open beach was patrolled on horseback by the aptly named 'Horse Marines'. The war may have been distant and abstract for much of America but on the Long Beach Peninsula it was not only real but on their doorstep.

Sally was twelve years old when war was declared. She was tall, curvatious, brunette, and buxom well beyond her years. Marguerite's nightmare was a welcome sight for the convoys of soldiers awaiting deployment who would drive past the Christie home daily. The attention of the young soldiers was appreciated and encouraged by the curious young bombshell. Sally and her friends never passed up an opportunity to visit the beach to ogle the handsome Horse Marines.

Patriotism was the order of the day. Every able-bodied male rushed to enlist even if he needed to lie about his age to be accepted. There was no sight more appealing to the girls and women of America than a man in uniform. Even ultra-reserved Margarite couldn't deny her attentions to the warriors who would defend our country in faraway foreign lands. She would serve coffee, tea, or whatever could be mustered, to the soldiers who found their way to her doorstep and with her overly endowed, brunette bombshell daughter waving to the passing convoys, it was a certainty many young men would find their way back to the Christie home in Nahcotta.

Soldiers brought cigarettes for Bill as an excuse to visit with Sally and Chris. Chris's soldier boyfriend smuggled sugar for the Christie's from the supply rooms of the military base. Many commodities were scarce necessitating rations to be placed on items and imposed onto the citizens to benefit the war effort. The final war to end all wars required a commitment by all. World War Two would prove to be the last time an entire population would rally with one voice. Dissenting voices disappeared as the American naval warships slipped beneath the waves in Pearl Harbor.

Margarite's war was much more personal. How could she stem the tide of soldiers who were interested in her twelve year old daughter who looked as if she were eighteen? She soon realized she could not, so her final tactic was to chaperone Sally so the naïve girl would not be alone with an older, more experienced man.

Ray was one such soldier, an enlistee who showed a keen, undeterred interest in young Sally. They would discover later Ray was twenty eight years old. Margarite drove Ray and Sally to the movie house in Illwaco.

Margarite sat directly behind the couple, missing the movie as her eyes never left her daughter.

Sally wasn't thinking of her mother seated behind them. Sally's blossoming body was awake like never before. When she allowed Ray to take her hand an avalanche of tingles rushed through her body. Every time he squeezed her hand heat waves washed over her. Ray took a prominent place in the memories of her march toward womanhood. Ray gave Sally her first romantic, adult kiss. It would never be forgotten. Ray's embrace was worlds beyond the stolen inquisitive kiss she and friend John shared in a closet when Sally was eight years old.

A world war dictated the mood of the planet but Sally's world was on the Long Beach Peninsula. Though her world was decorated with handsome soldiers her daily life required most of her time. There were chores. There was school. There were still trips to the Shriners Hospital. There was no war time out from polio. That too would change.

Sally's body and unstoppable spirit continued to grow. As with her earlier years, the one sure way to ensure she would do something was to tell her she couldn't. Opinions and directions from parents, teachers, neighbors, or doctors meant nothing to Sally. There were 140 million people in America but Sally listened to only one. Her conviction was a certainty based on an absolute; all choices in life were hers alone.

At fourteen years of age Sally was at the Shriners Hospital for what would be a final visit. Dr. Lucius Delahunt led Sally, her parents, and three other doctors into a conference room. His expression, as well as his colleagues was grim wrapped in serious. The tension sucked the air from the room as everyone took a seat.

Dr. Delahunt looked intently at Sally to assure her attention was his. His voice was the soothing tone bred of many bedsides. "Sally, we've come to an end of what we can do for you at this facility. Your legs are as strong as they can possibly become and, as always, your attitude is exemplary. There are other treatments available at specialized care facilities in different cities around the country but in my professional opinion the results would be minimal if any benefit at all. That reality leads us to where we are today.

I want you to know what the future holds for you. I don't want to alarm you but neither do I want to fill you with unrealistic expectations. There is no reason you can't live a relatively normal life but there will be certain limitations you will encounter. If you will consistently wear the leg braces, you should be able to maintain mobility for some time but you should expect to be restricted to a wheelchair by the time you're forty years old.

When the time comes to seek employment, you should look for a job in which you can remain seated for much of the work day. Avoid strenuous exercise and activities with the possible exception of swimming.

It's important you not allow yourself to get pregnant. It is my professional opinion you might transmit your disease to your off spring. Women with polio have successfully given birth without complications but I believe your body will not be capable of carrying a fetus to full term. I don't want to alarm you, Sally. You can still lead a rich, full life but you must accept your limitations. Because you possess a handicap does not make you different than others; you merely have restrictions due to your disease. Your attitude has always been exemplary, but please heed my words. Do you understand the importance of what I'm telling you? Any questions?"

Sally surveyed the sullen faces staring at her. Even her narcissistic mother pulled back her own ego and agendas to shed a tear upon hearing her daughter's grim prognosis. How was Sally supposed to react when the experts tell her she is doomed to always be different? Should she view the happiness of others and accept happiness was beyond her grasp? Dr. Delahunt's words haunted Sally for many weeks. His warnings echoed while she milked and staked the cow. They hung heavy on her young shoulders while she fed the chickens and collected their eggs. She thought of little else as she was stringing oyster shells for two cents per eight foot string to earn money for school clothes. Her first year of high school was quickly approaching.

Sally weighed all her options. She gave due consideration to Dr. Delahunt's warning. She arrived at a decision; doctors know medicine, teachers know education, parents know family, but only Sally knew Sally.

The school bus to Illwaco High School was scheduled to pick up handicapped Sally at her front door. She begged and pleaded with her mother to allow her to meet the bus at the bus stop with the other kids. Margarite relented to quiet her persistent daughter.

The first day of high school arrived and Sally stood proudly with all the other kids at the bus stop. Her leg braces were nowhere to be seen. They were neatly covered by tarpaper behind a blackberry bush between the Christie house and the bus stop. Sally told her teachers and her classmates she had been cured. She played baseball, tennis, and kick the can. She ran, rode bikes, and danced. Sally decided she was no longer handicapped.

Her diagnosis was working perfectly. Chris wouldn't tell Mom under threat from her newly cured little sister. Margarite discovered Sally's deception only because a teacher unknowingly congratulated Mom on Sally's miraculous recovery. It was just as well. The leg braces were rusting from spending every day outside in the elements of the rainy Northwest.

Margarite protested but in uncharacteristic fashion relented. Sally walked fine without the braces and never complained of pain. Mom agreed to let her daughter get on with her life. Marguerite was a teetotaling, tyrannical, religious zealot. What she was not, was stupid. She knew Sally was going to do as she damned well pleased the moment she was out of view. Headstrong is a descriptive term for most, in regards to Sally it was a character trait. She completely agreed with the experts; her life would not be ordinary. She determined it would be extraordinary.

Sally and her disease-free body set about the business of life. The war still raged in Europe and the Pacific which meant the Horse Marines were still patrolling the beach. She never passed an opportunity to cruise the beach, telling Mom she and her friends were looking for ornamental glass balls in the piles of bull kelp scattered around the beach. The glass balls rode the ocean currents from Japan and Okinawa where they'd broken free of the local's fishing nets.

One day Sally and two female friends were digging through an unusually large clump of kelp in search of glass balls when they discovered a grim reminder of war. They came upon the bloated, smelly corpse of a Japanese sailor entangled in the kelp. Her two friends were horrified at the repulsive sight. Sally saw only the opportunity to flag down a handsome Horse Marine. The sailor undoubtedly signed on to serve. He might as well serve as eye candy for Sally as his patriotic act.

Lee and Anne Wiegert lived close to the Christie's. Lee and Sally were best of friends. They were constant companions on the tennis court. Their friendship would remain strong, only coming into question once when he dared make a pass at her while parked at the lake; a pass she quickly rebuffed. Lee's mother was the worst, constantly pressuring Lee to marry Sally. The thought was ridiculous to Sally as she explained to

Lee's mother time and again. Lee was more brother than husband. Lee was her friend in the neighborhood but he was sent away to a religious academy for schooling. It didn't matter, Sally was happy at Illwaco High School.

Academics remained a pursuit for others but high school brought to bear a talent she had always possessed, Sally could sing. Not carry a pleasant tune around the campfire singing but rattle the window frames of the chorus room singing. The milk cow, chickens, herons, gulls, and any neighbor or passing oyster boat had known of Sally's talent for a long while but only once had someone who could have helped her with her passion offered encouragement. Sally's aunt could plainly hear the raw talent in her niece. Her aunt was a close friend of a voice teacher and offered to arrange an audition for Sally. Her aunt was enthusiastic, planting thoughts of Sally eventually attending the Julliard School of Music in New York City. She told Margarite her daughter possessed a rare talent and should be encouraged to develop that talent. Margarite refused the offer. She would not allow Sally to even audition for the voice teacher.

Margarite could prevent her daughter from traveling for voice lessons but no one would ever prevent her from singing. Sadly,

Sally's ability was overlooked even at school; the chorus teacher going so far as to make her sing alone in the auditorium so she wouldn't drown out the voices of her classmates. And sing Sally did, unrepentant, with all the passion she possessed. Audiences are unnecessary when you sing for yourself.

Time marched along and Sally followed to the personal beat of her private drum. One hot, humid summer day found Sally working at her household chores. She was appropriately dressed in a mud spattered, long sleeve, button down shirt complete with dungarees covered in chicken crap. Her hair was covered with a red bandanna. She wore rubber boots on her feet and yellow rubber gloves. It was the outfit any young girl hopes to be wearing when she sees a heart stopping vision. His name was Henry Heiss. He was visiting Chris along with another friend. Hank, as he was known, moved to Long Beach a month earlier from Milwaukee, Wisconsin.

Sally saw him again at the Siberian, a teen hang out in Long Beach. Saturday night was dance night at the Siberian and, occasionally, Margarite would take her two daughters, though, she stayed around to keep an eye on their activities. Margarite and Sally were leaning on the rail watching all the teens bopping around the dance floor when Sally spotted Hank dutifully dancing with his sister, Trudy.

Sally pointed to the handsome young man. She informed her mother, "I'm going to marry that man."

Margarite scoffed, as did Lee when Sally repeated her prediction. Lee, still harboring a hidden passion for Sally, went so far as to fix Hank up on a date with Doris Atwood in an attempt to derail Sally's plans. She was angry enough to spit nails at Lee but no matter. The game was only beginning. The world would learn; Sally gets Sally wants.

Chapter 5

Maggie pushed away from the desk. "She's a pistol alright but I still don't understand what she has to do with Zap. Do you think she was paying him to ghost write her story?"

"I doubt it," shrugged Zevon. "Something got to him. If it was just business that wouldn't explain the letter he wrote to you. I wonder how much of it is real and how much is from Zap's imagination. Sally might be a real person but the story could be all fiction."

Maggie smirked, "We'll never know."

A broad, wicked smile spread over Zevon's tanned face. "The hell we won't. Almost all municipal records were transferred to microfilm and then computerized. The paper's researchers are maestros at obtaining records. There have only been a few times they couldn't find something I asked for." Zevon flipped his cell phone open again. "Gladys, Zevon. I have a few more items I need. Yes, it's about Zap. I need school records from Illwaco High School in Washington State in 1944, '45, or thereabouts, for Sally Christie, or possibly Sara Christie." He paused for a second, "Just to be sure, check Betty Christie and while you're at it check a Hank Heiss, Henry I think it was. Then I need you to check the Shriners Hospital in Portland, Oregon from around 1935 to 1942 for the same girl. Last one; see when the ceremony for the grand opening of the Bonneville Dam took place. There should be lots of photos in news archives. FDR was there so there might be something in presidential records. I'm looking for a picture of the President with a little girl in a wheelchair at the ceremony. That's it. Thanks, Gladys. Call me on my cell phone."

Maggie sipped her wine glass. "Do you really think she can find all that?"

"Absolutely." He replied. "Gladys isn't by herself. She has an entire staff that is the best in the business. I'll bet she calls in less than ten minutes. I hope she can find a news photo from the ceremony. That would be awesome."

Maggie stood and walked slowly around the room, pausing at the different framed movie posters. Zevon surveyed his old friend. She was still the same heart stopper he remembered from college. Her frame was filled out from her coed days, mature but still trim and shapely. He could tell inside the tailored pantsuit she was fuller through the hips than in earlier years. Maybe she'd had a child? He had neglected to ask. Was she even married or did she have a boyfriend? Zevon struggled to see the importance in other people's lives, even old friends.

"So are you married, Mags?" He asked.

She turned with a grin. Her haunting emerald eyes flickered evil. "Why, you looking for a date?"

Zevon held his hands up as defense. "Not me. You're way too smart for me. Like I said, I like my women just smart enough to dress themselves. I was curious, that's all. You do look great though, Mags."

Her smile let him off the hook. "So do you, Z, but you've always known that. No, I'm not seeing anyone right now. I broke up four months ago with the guy I've been with for the last two years."

"What happened?" Zevon inquired. He didn't actually care but he was trying to conduct a conversation. Normally when Zevon feigned interest in a woman it was to get her naked.

Maggie chuckled, seeing instantly through his phony offer of interest. "You're still a pig. I broke up with him because he was too much like you and Zap."

He nodded, "You're right about me but Zap really was in love with you."

Maggie interrupted, "Zap was never in love with anyone. He thought the world and all its inhabitants were a boring waste. He was the smartest person I've ever known and he was as indifferent to himself as he was to me. Zap was an enigma wrapped in a shrug."

"But that's exactly what made him so good. Zap saw everything from a perspective no one else could find and his dark humor and biting sarcasm had people begging for more. Why do you think I've been riding his coattails since high school? Hell, Zap wrote more of my papers than I did. Remember the term paper I got published? The one that was probably responsible for the job I have today? It was all Zap; I didn't contribute a single syllable."

Maggie wasn't surprised by Zevon's confession. Zap made pocket money at NYU writing compositions for wayward wealthy students. There was more than one 'A' on papers in Maggie's university records which sprang from Zap's creative genius. "No one ever disputed Zap's intelligence; it was his capacity for love that was in question. He had as much compassion for everyone in the world as you do for obese chicks. That's why I'm stumped about Zap and this Sally woman in the story. I can't see an old woman breaking through Zap's armor. Maybe it's just my ego talking because I couldn't get through to him. If Sally is the woman he was talking about in the letter, I don't know if I should love or hate her."

Zevon's phone rang. "Yeah. Okay. Okay. All right. Really. What year was that? Can we get an original of that? Okay. Okay. Thanks, Gladys. I'll probably need you some more today. I'm not sure yet. I'll let you know. Thanks again."

Maggie's impatience wouldn't allow her to wait while he digested Gladys' newest information. "What is it? What did she find?"

Zevon turned, "Interesting. Sally and Hank graduated from Illwaco High School, him in 1942, her in 1946. Sally was definitely at the Shriners Hospital for treatment. She was there well over thirty times between 1935 in 1942. She was there for operations on two occasions and for a two year stretch, she went once a month. When Bonneville had its grand opening, Sally was at the hospital. Gladys found lots of photos of FDR but only one where there's a glimpse of another wheelchair in the crowd but she said you couldn't tell if it's a little girl. The interesting part is in a story from the Seattle Intelligencer. They mentioned an exchange between the president and a member of the audience which caused a momentary stir but they didn't elaborate. That could have been our Sally."

Maggie smiled at the passage in Zap's story, "Let's read some more."

Chapter 6

The way to a man's heart is through his stomach or so the wisdom of the day stated. Sally could work shoulder to shoulder with any man. She could defend herself with her fists. She could sing like an operatic angel. She could string spat at the oyster yard with a smile on her face and mud in her hair. What Sally Christie could not do was cook. Lack of culinary skills would normally be a problem but Sally figured she'd take it one step at a time. The goal was to impress Hank with her expertise in the kitchen. Phase one was to find out his favorite dishes. Apple pie was the consensus so apple pie would be Sally's initial foray into the joy of cooking. For three days she toiled, tossing failed attempt after failed attempt into the garbage before finally serving Hank her apple pie which she assured him was but one of her specialties. The circle was complete. Hank had found a beautiful, fun-loving young woman who could cook like a gourmet chef. Nothing could be more perfect. Hank and Sally officially became an item.

The war had ended and optimism was the order of the day in every corner of the country. Citizens and soldiers rallied as one making America safe from oppression. America was a world leader and the people shared in her glory.

Hank served as an interpreter for military intelligence in the European theatre of operations. His parents were German immigrants who settled in Milwaukee in the 1920's. German was the spoken language in the Heiss household so Hank was quite fluent. He also scored extremely high on military aptitude tests so he was quickly in demand once deployed. Rumor on the Long Beach Peninsula were Hank was an interpreter on the staff of General Patton. It remained rumor since humble Hank resisted speaking of the war in any respect. Though he didn't like talking about his war experience he shared one story with his young girlfriend and later with a female reporter who was writing an article about the war.

Hank's unit was temporarily stationed on the outskirts of a quaint German village. An American soldier had gone missing and the Military Police sent into the village could not locate nor find even word of him. Hank, being fluent in the local language, was given the task of going amongst the villagers to try to discover the fate of the lost soldier.

Hank returned four days later with the location of the man in question. In truth, he found the wayward soldier within hours of entering the town but since he wasn't given a specific timetable to accomplish the task, he decided to enjoy the food, beer, and company of the local frauliens; a tiny detail he failed to mention to his superior officer. No harm, no foul.

Back on the peninsula, Hank and Sally were riding the wave of young love. Following the war and the Great Depression money was tight so date options for the couple would consist of a coin flip to decide whether to eat or enjoy a movie in Illwaco. There was always 'Amos and Andy', 'Fibber, McGee, and Molly', 'The Shadow' or other radio programs on the porch of the Christie house. Also there was Long Beach and you never knew what might be happening or what you might find on the beach.

Bill once found enough lumber washed ashore from a passing freighter to build a garage. Another time hundreds of sacks of flour landed on the beach. The outer layer were salt water encrusted but inside was perfectly usable flour. Hank's best catch happened when a floundering freighter lost a cargo of beer. He'd idle his Model A on the beach while hanging out the driver's side door scooping and tossing beers into the backseat. He collected enough to build a towering pyramid on the back porch of his parent's house. The pyramid was an architectural masterpiece but Hank and his friends drank all the beer anyway.

Times were changing, even at the Christie household. Bill decided to retire the outhouse and install indoor plumbing for the family. Bill would finally be able to forget those late night trips in the pouring rain or the time he painted his butt red by taking a seat immediately after Sally painted the outhouse. Bill purchased a brand new toilet from Mr. Duper at the hardware store in Illwaco. Bill started digging a hole to install a septic tank but he encountered a pipe just below the surface. Following the underground pipe led him to a brand new septic tank which had been beside the house for all those many years while they dumped pots and trudged to the outhouse in every kind of weather.

Margarite was humiliated she'd spent so many years conducting her bodily functions in such unladylike fashion. Bill was amused, no reason for embarrassment. No one told him the septic tank was there when he bought the house so why should Margarite have expected him to know. Sally thought it was hilarious.

Many things and most people failed to conform to Margarite's vision of a perfect family unit or community. She would be a major obstacle for Hank and Sally's budding romance. Hank didn't seem to mind. He honorably served his country and didn't believe he owed explanations for his behavior, not even to Sally's mother. Though quiet and humble, Hank was a good looking, intelligent man's man. Many jealous female eyes followed Hank when he walked down the boulevard with Sally on his arm.

Hank knew of Marguerite's teetotalling ways so whenever he'd make the drive from Long Beach to Nahcotta to see Sally, he'd stop at the tavern for a drink before he arrived at the Christie house. Margarite was appalled her daughter's suitor would imbibe of Satan's elixir and made no effort to hide her scorn. Margarite finally asked Hank why he insisted upon going to the Devil's den. Hank shrugged and informed Margarite it was because he wanted a drink. On his next visit there was a six pack of beer in the ice box. Margarite might not convince him to avoid the drink but at least she could keep him out of the tavern.

The irony of Margarite's battle against alcohol was known to everyone but her. Bill hid his penchant for drink from his wife until the day he died. Years after Bill was gone, Sally and Chris would continue to find partially filled bottles of 'Old Grand Dad' whiskey hidden about the house and property.

Alcohol may have been Marguerite's battle but her identity she received through the church. There wasn't a Presbyterian church on the peninsula so Margarite, Chris, and Sally, if she could be corralled, faithfully attended the Methodist Church in Nahcotta. Marguerite's devotion to her faith would prove to be a major roadblock for Hank and Sally. Hank was a misbegotten Catholic, a fact Margarite could not tolerate.

The prediction Sally made to her mother and to Lee four years earlier was to come to fruition; Hank proposed to Sally. They were sitting in his car looking out over the oyster yard discussing Hank's tonsillectomy scheduled for the following day. Sally said she had secured use of the family car to go see Hank after his operation. Sally also told him she was experiencing an extremely painful earache.

Hank said," If we were married I could take care of you."

Sally quickly inquired," Was that a proposal?"

In Hank's unassuming manner, he shrugged," I guess it was."

Sally didn't make it to visit her fiancé the following day. She was bedridden, doing a respectable impersonation of a bullfrog; Sally had the mumps. Doctor Strang made a house call to check on Sally after removing Hank's tonsils. Hank didn't catch the mumps but he was hopelessly caught up with Sally.

The young couple was in love and engaged to be married. Differing faiths wasn't a barrier, religious differences hadn't stopped them from falling in love. Hank's mother, Frances, didn't present a problem. Frances thought Sally was the 'bees knees'. Margarite could only see her daughter standing at the gates of hell beside a barbarian Catholic.

Margarite would be an obstacle the two would need to confront but they faced another more immediate problem if they wanted to get married. Hank needed a career.

Hank had a standing offer of a good job from Reese Williams, the manager of the bank in Illwaco. Reese was enthusiastically recruiting Hank because he was intelligent and a quick study. Hank also looked dashing in a suit as well as being charming with the ladies. Finally, Hank's stand up character commanded respect from the men. He was exactly who Reese wanted for the bank.

Reese pushed hard but Hank had another dream for himself. He was very mechanical in nature and possessed a meticulous quality toward all projects he undertook, perfect traits for Hank's desire. He wanted to be a watchmaker. His problem was there were no watchmaking schools in his area.

Hank was industrious and hardworking but there was one quality he didn't possess. There was no project he could not accomplish once it was presented but Hank was not a self-starter. He needed a push in the necessary direction. Hank wanted to marry Sally Christie. He would never meet a woman more qualified to initiate that push.

Sally sent for the paperwork to secure funding for Hank's schooling through the newly created G.I. Bill. She then located and wrote to every watchmaking school in the country. She found only two immediate openings; one in San Antonio, Texas and one in Kansas City, Kansas. Hank told Sally, after boot camp, he never again wanted to step foot in the state of Texas, so Kansas City it was.

Phase one was complete. Phase two was acquiring parental approval from Sally's parents, which meant from Margarite. Sally was only seventeen years old. America was basking in the light of promise but the fledging superpower just emerged from a world war and the worst depression in American history. Marguerite was assured by the Kansas City Chamber of Commerce and the Housing Authority; the young couple would find it quite impossible to find housing in the Kansas City metropolitan area. Armed with that knowledge, Margarite agreed to sign for Sally if they could rent an apartment in Kansas City.

The stars were aligned against the two lovers. The economy conspired to squelch their marital plans and Hank's career. Margarite was convinced even her daughter's unbridled determination could not overcome reality from two thousand miles away. Margarite didn't take into account the X factor, Hank was horny.

Sally put her hormonally frustrated fiancé on the train with a mission, find an apartment. They'd underestimated a young man's libido. Hank quickly rented a room in a rundown boarding house. Young love had won out. Margarite was ready to concede defeat but she held one final card to play. Sally needed to attend a counseling session at her Methodist Church, supposedly for guidance to help with her upcoming married life.

Reverend Dickson was briefed by Margarite. His job was to convince Sally of the fallacy of young marriages surviving long term. Failing that he was going to cajole, shame, and as a last resort scare her into backing out of her plans. The good Reverend was prepared; he spewed logic and common sense. Sally wasn't budging. She informed Reverend Dickson, Hank was Catholic and she intended to raise her children Catholic.

The Reverend ceased pleading Margarite's agenda. His voice rose exponentially in volume; his tone turned to anger. He bellowed fire and brimstone ending with a growled warning, "If you marry this heretic Catholic, you will go straight to hell!"

Sally stood, smiling sweetly. She calmly replied, "I'll see you there." She left Reverend Dickson's office. Sally had a train to catch.

Her sister, once again Mary Jane since reaching adulthood, accompanied Sally to Kansas City. The two sisters found the term Hank used to describe the apartment, rundown, was flattering at best. The bathtub was in the hallway with a makeshift plywood wall around it. If you stood up in the tub you could converse with whoever might be in the hallway. They learned quickly if they heard papers rustling around the icebox at night, come out throwing knives so the rodents didn't think they could intimidate you. Hank and Sally called them hot and cold running rats. The apartment was a dive by any definition. It was dark, damp, dingy, and drafty but they were in love. It was perfect.

Mary Jane stood up for Sally and the two love birds were married by a justice of the peace at the Kansas City courthouse. They took a quick honeymoon to Hank's hometown of Milwaukee, the honeymoon capital of eastern Wisconsin, before returning to the sanctity of their dive.

Their newfound joy evaporated when they opened the door to their apartment. Everything they owned was gone: the bedding, dishes, towels, their clothing, even the wedding gifts Sally and Mary Jane hauled on the train from Nahcotta.

The landlady, a kindhearted woman named Sheridan, found them staring in shock at the barren room. It seemed a larger room became available while they were in Milwaukee so Sheridan, trailed closely by her overfed dog Bum, moved all of their worldly possessions to the larger room. Not only did she move them, but Sheridan put everything away and even made the bed. The rooming house may have been a dump but Sheridan was a gem, even if her dog resembled the hot and cold running rats.

Hank and Sally Heiss began the rigors of daily life. Hank attended Watchmaking School at night and Sally secured a receptionist job at TransWorld Airways. Every morning Sally would find a yellow rose, her favorite, on the table which Hank handpicked for her on his way home from school. The yellow rose appeared every day the couple lived in Kansas City.

Life wasn't all roses for young love. They lived in a seedy section of the city. One night Sally was heating water on the stove to wash dishes when she saw a man lurking on the fire escape. She threw the pot of scalding water through the window and with an agonizing scream the intruder changed his mind, running away. After that encounter Hank transferred to day classes.

Watchmaking School was everything Hank believed it would be. He was fascinated by the tiny precision gears, levers, springs, and pendulums. He marveled at the way the precision machined pieces meshed to create a working timepiece. Hank excelled at discovering the flaws and deficiencies of a broken movement. Minute detail was something his eye was born to embrace. Hank and a fellow student, Jake, outpaced the other students in no time so the instructors begin utilizing their skills to repair watches for local jewelers.

Jake and wife Rebecca were from Georgia where Jake's father owned a jewelry store which explained why Jake excelled at Watchmaking School. The school's instructors informed Hank and Jake their level of proficiency would allow them to graduate earlier than their classmates. In addition, if they could provide a letter stating they were going to a job at a reputable jeweler, they could also keep their tools at the expense of the G.I. Bill.

Jake's father supplied a letter and within days he and Rebecca were gone. Hank was sad to see his friend leave but Hank didn't have a job to go to. He returned to repairing watches, alone, for the school.

Sally inquired as to exactly what the letter Hank needed would be required to say. She didn't have any second thoughts about leaving her job at TWA. She wasn't cut out for reception work at a corporate office. Only once did something even remotely exciting happen during her work day. It happened shortly after TWA was purchased by Howard Hughes. Sally's supervisor called to tell her one of Mr. Hughes' representatives was coming and she was to show him into the room containing the tickertape machines. A well-dressed man with a pencil mustache approached her desk and asked for directions to the tickertape room. Sally escorted him and waited while he checked all the tapes in the room. On his way out he surprised her by patting her on the butt.

"Thank you, sweetheart," he said before disappearing down the hallway. She found out the man was not a representative but the man himself. It isn't every day the richest man in the country slaps you on the ass.

Hank put his head down, determined to finish school. Sally had other ideas. She would return to the Northwest and find a job for Hank. No matter it was the 1940's and, aside from Rosie the Riveter who retired at the end of the war, a woman's place was in the home not pounding the streets searching for a job for her husband.

The school administrator said she'd be wasting her time. Sheridan told her it couldn't be done. Mary Jane said she was crazy. There was only one thing left to do; Sally boarded a train, leaving Hank with two shirts, two pairs of pants, and underwear. She left one cooking pan, plate, glass, knife, fork, and spoon. The one task she avoided, she didn't call her mother.

Sally called her mother from the train station in Astoria. Margarite drove to pick up her daughter. Her first words when she saw Sally were, "If you left Hank you might as well get back on the train." Mom convinced herself on the drive to Astoria the only reason for an untimely return was Sally must be pregnant.

When Sally told her why she returned, Margarite joined the chorus of others telling Sally there was no possible way she would find a job for Hank.

It seemed others might finally be correct, there were challenges Sally could not defeat. Astoria, Warrenton, Seaside, Chinook, Illwaco, Long Beach, Ocean Park, Raymond, South Bend. Sally was scoffed at, laughed at, and chastised for her temerity. Common sense should have ended Sally's fruitless mission. She decided to widen the search. Her Aunt Anne offered a room in Seattle and Sally was on the bus.

Two weeks passed while Sally pounded the sidewalks of Seattle. The results were similar to what she'd experienced back home, only now inflected with big city arrogance. Still, every morning she'd rise and open the doors of every jewelry store and jewelry counter she could find. Sally was reaching another crossroads in her search; she was running out of places to look for work. She would either have to finally admit defeat or move on to another city.

As a last desperate attempt, Aunt Anne said she'd try to arrange a meeting with

Fred Frost, a man she knew only in passing. She thought he was a jeweler or at least she'd heard his name mentioned in conversations about jewelry.

Fred Frost was indeed a jeweler. Sally met him to plead her case. Fred was moved by the young woman's spunk, determination, and sincerity. Sally assured Fred if Hank wasn't everything she'd proclaimed he could fire him on the spot. Fred gave Sally the letter she needed. Ten days later Hank and his tools were in Seattle.

Chapter 7

Maggie raised her brow. "When you think about the time when Sally was doing these things, it's amazing how bold she was. Still, I can't for the life of me see how it would have interested Zap. He didn't write biographies and even if he did, why her? Why not someone famous or at least someone we'd heard of. I've never heard of her, have you?"

Zevon shrugged. "Not before today. I can see why people would be interested. What a fireball. When Sally was knocking on doors, I was thinking what I would do if some woman came to my office looking for a job for her husband. I'd laugh her out of my office and still be laughing over drinks that night. I would figure the guy was a total flake. That's now. She was doing this shit sixty years ago. She had cajones. No wonder Hank fell for her. He must have been some kind of stud or she would have probably killed him on the honeymoon."

Maggie went into the kitchen to refill her wineglass with water from the tap. "What do you say we order out for something to eat? I know I'm not leaving until I get through Sally's story."

Zevon pulled his cell phone from his pocket, dialing a number from the speed dial to order Chinese take-out.

Maggie reread Zap's letter. She was still in disbelief about the words he intended to send to her.

Zevon hung up the phone. He could see Maggie's mind was still on Sally. "I'm starting to get a kick out of Sally's story. If we verify the legitimacy of it, there's no reason why we couldn't have it published. There should be one book in the world with the name Zap O'Brien on it." Zevon held up the bottle of wine to Maggie.

Maggie declined with a shake of her head before responding, "Aren't you getting a little ahead of yourself? I haven't read as much of Zap's work as you, but he always wrote a first draft extremely fast. It was raw but he said it was honest that way. Then he'd go back to polish and expand on whatever he was writing. This story seems pretty first draft me. I mean, there's passion and emotion but there's very little dialogue. It's heavy on fact and light on description. How do you propose to get around that?"

Zevon shrugged, "Easy. Remember, I have access to an entire staff of writers and editors. Sure this is a first draft but so far the story appears to be all there. You are right, Zap still pours out a first draft extremely fast. Sometimes it's scary, he gets so involved. He'll stop blinking and even quits breathing at times. Even though this story needs editing, it's different for Zap but different in a good way. He's pulling from Sally's spirit and her personality. Usually he only pries into people's dark side. I'm excited about where he's going and, honestly, Sally kind of intrigues me. I don't know about you but its kind of fun getting verification about her life. Do you want to keep going?"

Maggie studied his carefully cultured, pretty boy persona look. No doubt Zevon still melted hearts. His college dorm room could have supplied the script and talent for a few dozen 'B' porn movies. "Sure, I'm not ready to quit reading. I want to know how the story ends. Don't think I'm going to get drunk so you can add my name to the list of women whose names you can't remember."

Zevon flashed his movie star smile. "Is that why you quit drinking? You have nothing to worry about. Tonight I want to chase Zap's mind not your body. I'll admit I followed you to the student union that day we met, it wasn't a chance meeting. I'll further admit when you told me to keep my nickel slick dick in my pants, I introduced you to Zap so I could get another shot at you but when you two hit it off, the door slammed shut. You were Zap's girl and that's how it'll stay.

Aren't you curious what it is about this woman that got to him? I can't believe it. You're the only one I ever saw get to him but even you couldn't change him. Sally must be a witch or something."

Maggie held her wine glass of tap water as a toast. "I'm with you. Where do we go next?"

The cell phone came out, "Gladys, Zevon. I need you to check marriage licenses in Kansas City, Missouri. Let me see, she was seventeen so it had to be 1945 or '46. Also check the enrollees at a watchmaking school in Kansas City at the same time. We're looking for Henry or Hank Heiss and if possible a guy named Jake from Georgia. There was a rooming house; the manager's name was Sheridan. Could be a first or last name. Then go to Seattle. We're looking for a jeweler named Fred Frost." Zevon was silent for a moment. "Nothing like that. It's from something Zap was working on before he died. We don't know yet where it fits or if it does. I promise I'll let you know as soon as we figure it out. I know how close you were. Thanks, Gladys. I'll wait for your call."

Maggie inquired, "She and Zap were close? Was it your kind of close?"

Zevon enthusiastically shook his head. "No way. Gladys is close to sixty years old with grandkids. She's built for research not lust. But she's awesome at her job. Zap depended on Gladys to fill in all the blanks."

"Well, Sally's old. Maybe Zap's taste in women has changed," She said with equal parts sarcasm and regret.

"No, Mags. You cured him of smart women but he still liked them age appropriate." Zevon lifted his glass in an attempt to stall her and change the subject. He tried putting the topic to rest, "I would have bet on you, Mags. If anyone was going to change him, I would have figured it would have been you and I was hoping you wouldn't. I'm a self-centered, selfish bastard and I wanted Zap in my life, not yours. He was my mentor, friend, wingman, and the only person in the world who didn't judge me. Zap didn't expect anything from me, just for me to be there if he needed me. I respected him for that. Not many people could remain friends for so long with someone who lives in the shallow end of the pool like me."

Zevon's phone rang. "Yeah, Gladys. Good. Okay. That's all, huh? Nothing. Too bad. Okay. Thanks, I'll get back to you." He turned to Maggie. "Henry and Sara Heiss were married in Kansas City in 1946. He was enrolled in the Kansas School of Watchmaking. There were two students with the first name Jake but their hometown records no longer exist. Gladys couldn't find anything on a boarding house with an owner named Sheridan but she's still searching. Fred Frost was a jewelry wholesaler who did overflow watch repairs for the larger jewelers in the Seattle area. Well, at least we're in Seattle. Let's see what Sally does in Seattle."

Chapter 8

The only question about Sally's talent level would be in regard to the opportunities she was presented to showcase her ability. From the early days when she serenaded the milk cow and the chickens to the days when the chorus teacher separated her from classmates, there was one consensus; the girl could sing.

Margarite wanted another dotting, dutiful daughter like Chris. What she got was a tomboy with a pinup body and the spirit of a wildcat. Marguerite was able to stifle opportunities for Sally to advance her talents but no one would ever prevent her from singing. She would simply go out back and sing to the livestock with every ounce of vocal strength she could summon and when sent to the gymnasium at Illwaco High, she climbed to the top of the bleachers and blew the dust from the rafters.

Most call it luck, but in Sally's life, luck usually took a backseat to willpower. Was it luck she survived polio? Was it luck she married her number one fan? Was it luck career brought them to Seattle? No matter, once settled Hank encouraged Sally to seek avenues to do what she loved to do, sing and entertain.

It was that aspect, entertainment, which was the X factor taking Sally's already exceptional talent to stratospheric heights. Every generation has talented singers no one will ever hear because that special quality which drives people to want to see them perform is missing. There's an extra gene not in their makeup, a gene that lights an inner glow when an audience is present. These wanton souls lose themselves in the back row of church choirs or waste their skills in the shower.

The others, like Sally, come alive when there is someone to share with. Their bodies contain an extra gear, driving them to please adoring eyes. It can be seen in the flame of the eyes and the passion of the movements. A singer's voice can fill a room. The energy of an entertaining singer will consume a room.

Ego will prevent some talents from putting forth a supreme effort unless the audience is of sufficient size. They can only see themselves in a big room. For Sally a packed auditorium received the very same effort and emotion as the milk cow. It was about the singing. When there was an audience of one or a thousand, they got entertaining Sally and they got all of her.

Finding the venues to sing was difficult. Most who heard Sally sing immediately wanted to hitch to her wagon but the entertainment world revolves on an axis of ego. There is rampant greed, jealousy, and unknown numbers whose only purpose is to use others for their own benefit. Sally never succumbed to the lure of the casting couch. Sally just wanted to sing.

Sally sang with the local big bands at the Elks club. She sang in piano bars throughout the Seattle region. She sang with the Seattle Philharmonic and performed at the University of Washington series of Broadway shows. In 1962, Sally sang with the Joe Vanutti orchestra at the Diamond Horseshoe club on the strip at the World's Fair. Through a classified ad notifying the public of auditions for singers, Sally found John Andrews. John was an extremely talented man who directed a traveling troupe, performing assorted works like those of Gilbert and Sullivan at venues from civic auditoriums to high school gymnasiums.

The productions thrived on the strength of the vocals because they couldn't afford an entire band so John was the only accompaniment on piano. He was an accomplished pianist and a wonderful director who managed to bring out the best of his cast. John, like Sally, possessed the talent to flourish in any market which presented an opportunity but his family obligations kept him, quite happily, on the small stage close to home.

The complicated arrangements of a Gilbert and Sullivan production were a new challenge for Sally. Though some numbers would be daunting, Sally possessed the range and determination to master the songs in a manner which would have pleased the composers. From 'Madame Butterfly' to her favorite production 'Patience', Sally sang them all. The powerful operatic pipes that shook the windows in high school were now controlled and polished.

Audiences left a John Andrews production thrilled with the show but awed at Sally's performance. The same words were on many lips, 'why wasn't this woman on the big stage'? Broadway, Hollywood, Carnegie Hall, The Met? Sally had the pipes to sing anywhere. What the audiences couldn't know was she didn't care. Singers who sing because of their passion, sing for themselves. Audiences were witnesses along for the ride. If celebrity arrived it would be delivered by the hands of others. Meanwhile, people would have the pleasure of hearing her sing. Number one fan, Hank, was always in the front row unless he watched his wife from the wings because John had enlisted his help building sets.

People were listening, even when Sally didn't realize they were listening. One evening after rehearsal, she was driving home alone and, as always, she was singing. Sally didn't sing in hushed tones. Red lights appeared behind her car. She was, at first, alarmed hoping she hadn't driven through a red light or some other traffic offense while lost in song.

A highway patrolman sauntered to the driver's side window. He paused at the window while Sally frantically prepared an apology for her lack of concentration on her driving. The patrolman leaned in. "I'm sorry I had to stop you, ma'am, but I heard you singing when you came off the freeway. I had to tell you how wonderful you sound."

The patrolman, like so many others after hearing Sally, knew they'd witnessed something special but it can be difficult to put a finger on the why? What makes one version of a song better than another? Why does one production linger in the memory while another doesn't? The answer is as elusive as the memory. You experience passion, you don't explain it. Pleasure isn't to be witnessed; it washes over you as a gentle wave. Sally's sweet power would caress ears but it was an unseen spirit which touched their hearts. In a world of false promises and prepackaged celebrity, Sally was truly real.

Sally performed for years with John Andrews as well as any other venue which arose to share her talent. Life always finds another obstacle for testing resolve. Sally's test was a direct assault on one of the true joys in her life.

On a day like all others, Sally rose in the morning but when she opened her mouth to sing there was nothing, no sound at all. No matter how hard she tried, no matter how much effort she exerted, not a sound emerged. Only a singer would understand the panic which gripped Sally.

The doctor easily diagnosed her problem. Sally had polyps on her vocal cords preventing them from vibrating to create song. The operation to correct the problem was straightforward but still dangerous. Sally lingered on the danger aspect for a micro second before agreeing to the operation. In her mind, losing her voice was akin to losing a limb and the fear of losing her limbs already slowed her life for a micro second.

The operation was performed with a medical student audience. Sally always did best with an audience. All went without complications and she emerged unscathed, though, the doctor's instructions telling her not to utter a sound for two weeks was like telling her to stop breathing or to juggle chainsaws.

Recovery went well and she and Hank went to the doctor's office for the final prognosis. In a scene eerily reminiscent of a meeting from years before at the Shriners Hospital, a team of medical experts laid out the latest set of restrictions life was offering. Sally would fully recover but she wouldn't sing again. Scar tissue on her vocal cords would prevent her returning to her former vocal self. Also, they informed her she should immediately cease smoking. Sally had never smoked a cigarette in her life. Secondhand smoke was a concept not recognized until decades later but she was living proof of the damage incurred living with a smoker in addition to spending all those nights singing in smoky piano bars.

Opera singers fade away when they are no longer capable of reaching the required notes at the top of the musical scale. At last a doctor gave a warning to Sally she couldn't defeat. She would never sing Gilbert and Sullivan or Opera again.

Depression was a word packed away with can't and don't. The doctors said Sally wouldn't sing again. They didn't say she shouldn't. Her once powerful voice with unlimited range lost two full octaves from the upper range but the power remained. The answer to losing a portion of her voice was simple; transform.

'Frivolous Sal' was born. Instead of opera and the classics it was fun songs, bold and bawdy songs. Sally quickly discovered bawdy was a lot more fun. Singing opera required reaching for the audience through the strength of the performance. Frivolous and brash allowed the audience to become part of the performance. Sally continued marching to her own tune, only now it had a different, bawdy drumbeat.

Audiences would again marvel at Sally's talent but it was the charisma that propelled them from their seats. Once again there were whispers, 'why wasn't she on a bigger stage?' There were opportunities, three to be exact.

The World's Fair came to Seattle in 1962. The Washington city would be showcased on the biggest stage on the planet. Every business in town endeavored to cash in on the opportunity. Seattle's Space Needle was an engineering marvel; built for the World's Fair, the Space Needle would become the symbol of the city of Seattle, recognized the world over for the years long after the World's Fair was gone.

On Pier 36 a group of investors bankrolled the refurbishing of an 1800's style paddle boat as an upscale restaurant and showroom. The plan was to have the project finished before hundreds of thousands invaded Seattle for their cities' time in the spotlight. Sally was slated to be the hostess/greeter as well as the headlining entertainment. The whole world would be exposed to Sally's rousing energy and entertaining style. The general manager sent her to be fitted for six extravagant evening gowns for her and the paddle boat's debut.

The excitement in the Heiss' household matched that of the entire city. Sally couldn't wait for the grand opening. The anticipation was so overwhelming she had trouble getting to sleep and when she did, dreams of overflow crowds and standing ovations filled her head. The long-awaited day drew near. One week before the grand opening two events would alter plans. One was front page news; the other was much more personal. The paddle boat sunk beneath the surface of Lake Union taking Sally's shot on the big stage down with it. Strike one.

Sally was running cocktails at the 40 and 8 Club when she met an entertainer named Dick Day. He was a talented man who traveled about from club to club, much in demand. He was performing at the club and while on break heard Sally sing a song for some persistent regular customers who loved to hear her vocal styling. Dick was highly impressed and without knowing anything else about her, asked if she would like to accompany him on a three-month long gig in Hawaii. They would perform at the top showrooms in the islands. Hank was all for the idea.

Sally met Dick at a local studio to begin rehearsing for their upcoming engagements. Dick told Sally he got his start and enthusiasm for entertaining while singing and playing organ at funerals. He'd never lost his love for the hymns. Dick asked if she knew 'In the Garden', his late father's favorite song. Sally said she did, so Dick sat down, started a tape recorder and motioned for her to begin.

She sang his request accappela and when finished, Dick sat speechless. Sally wasn't sure if he'd liked her rendition of his father's favorite song or not. When you sing a song familiar to the listener there is a risk your version might not appeal to the listener's ear. Being familiar with a song gives the listener an expectation of what they want to hear.

Dick smiled, tears coming to the corners of his eyes. "That was beautiful, Sally. I've never heard it better."

He rewound the tape and settled back to listen to Sally's beautiful voice once more. A tear broke free, gently sliding down his face. A quarter of the way through the heart wrenching song, Dick Day slumped over, quite dead. A definite strike.

Mickey Finn was a national personality and a Las Vegas mainstay. He and his show was a fixture at the Main Street Station on Fremont Street in the heart of sin city. Mickey was also a good friend of Red Watson, a honky-tonk banjo player from the old west streets of Virginia City, a lively tourist town revived of the silver mining days a century earlier. Red was a friend and frequently accompanied Sally and her bodacious singing styles. Red was convinced her bold style would be a perfect fit for Mickey Finn's show which was high energy and full of fun and fancy musical numbers. Red arranged an audition and, surprising no one, Mickey loved Sally. Mickey told her she was everything he was looking for in a female vocalist. The woman he currently employed had a contract set to expire in three months. He said he wanted Sally to replace her. Mickey sent her home with sheet music for the numbers she'd need to perform. They'd start rehearsals as soon as he was freed from his contractual commitment.

The Mickey Finn show in Las Vegas, the entertainment mecca of America, was a major opportunity. At last, huge audiences as well as the movers and shakers of entertainment would have the pleasure of enjoying Sally's infectious singing talent and show stopping charisma.

The name Sally Heiss would never grace a Las Vegas marquee. Three weeks before her debut the Main Street Station declared bankruptcy and closed the doors. Mickey Finn went back to Texas, promising Sally he'd call when he put together another production. Mickey didn't call. Sally went back to work. Three strikes you're out.

Chapter 9

There was genuine excitement in Zevon's voice, "Cool. We should be able to find all sorts of records about Sally's singing career. Wouldn't it be awesome to find a flyer or a promotional poster? Wouldn't you like to see what Sally looks like? I've got a mental sketch but they rarely turn out to be close to the reality."

His enthusiasm was beginning to infect Maggie. She wasn't sure whether it was curiosity about Sally or simply some innate desire to know how this mystery woman managed to breach the cynical defenses of Maggie's ex-husband. Either way, Sally and Zap's story needed a conclusion. "So what are you going to have Gladys look for?"

Zevon's phone buzzed with a text. He read it out loud. "Searched wrong state. Boarding house Kansas City, Kansas not Missouri. Main Street. Sheridan first name. Died 1964. G" His brown eyes reflected on Maggie's face, "What do you think? There should be all sorts of information about the World's Fair."

Maggie agreed, "Yes, and the same for the Philharmonic and the Broadway productions at the University. The Gilbert and Sullivan stuff sounds like community theater stuff so those records might not have made the jump to the latest technologies."

Zevon scrolled back a few pages before speed dialing Gladys, "It's me. Yeah, we're getting into it, too. What? Zap's ex-wife, Maggie. Yeah, that Maggie." He smiled, "Are you ready? I've got a lot this time. I hear you; I'd like to find a picture myself." Zevon nodded as he listened. He continued, "Too bad. Anyway, the '62 World's Fair. Sally sang with the Joe Vanutti Orchestra at the Diamond Horseshoe Club. She also performed with the Seattle Philharmonic. It would have been sometime in the '50s or '60s. Another venue was some Broadway productions at the University of Washington. Lastly, there was a guy named John Andrews who produced shows, Gilbert and Sullivan type stuff. Sally sang with him for a few years. I'm hoping someone scanned a flyer. Thanks, Gladys."

Maggie asked, "What was too bad?"

He thought for a moment, "Oh yeah. Gladys checked newspapers in and around Kansas City for '46 and '47, trying to find a wedding photo but she didn't find anything. She said public notices weren't published back then because they had to be copied and physically taken to the paper. Only the rich weddings made the papers."

She refilled her glass in the kitchen. The diversion provided by the tracking of Sally's life was welcome. Maggie didn't want to think about the reality of mortality. She'd spent four years sweeping Zap from her memory, having him suddenly thrust back into her life was confusing and unwanted. Zevon was part and parcel of those carefree times she'd relocated to the files of youthful indiscretion of the past. The last thing she wanted to do was reminisce about those days. They were gone and rightly so. Maggie was older with adult responsibilities and problems. As sad as the premature death of a young man is, even an ex-husband, there was little Maggie could do to alter or reconcile the reality of the situation. The dilemma she faced arose because she'd never managed to hate Zap; she simply recognized her life with him was an exercise in futility. Maggie couldn't envision a bright future with Zap, only life under a dark, cynical cloud which would only grow darker. Leaving Zap was not a move motivated by hatred or disdain but was bred of self-preservation. Zap was a gentle man capable of seeing only the sinister side of civilization so he lived there and wanted Maggie to live beside him. She wanted more for herself even if more was undefined and beyond her present field of vision.

Maggie asked a light question as a way to distract her train of thought, "Why did your parents name you Zevon? I mean, I know it was after some song, but why? Was the singer a friend or were they groupies or roadies or something?"

Zevon scoffed, "It wasn't anything profound or even interesting for that matter. The song was 'Werewolves of London' and his name was Warren Zevon and mine is the inverse, Zevon Warren. It may have been cute at cocktail parties when I was a baby and the song was on the charts but now it's just a forgettable quip about a strange old song and a weird name. My parents were like Zap's with selective memories when it comes to their past. Maybe Mom still listens when she's driving home to the Hamptons from her latest bout at the rehab clinic. And they wonder why their kids are misdirected and unhappy."

"Who says we're all unhappy?" Her grin was facetious and her eyes belied any disagreement with Zevon's assumption.

He shrugged, "So are you happy?"

Maggie wanted to bust his chops not reflect on her lot in life. "Define happiness. I don't laugh myself to sleep at night but I don't medicate myself unconscious either. Not yet anyway. I can't say life has turned out like I'd imagined but who can. The eight years I squandered with Zap weren't very helpful or memorable for that matter. I'm doing alright. I'll find my way."

Zevon smiled, "Not a glaring revue, Mags. Mine wouldn't be much different, though. At the rate I'm going I'll be carpooling with my mom to the rehab clinic by the time I'm forty. Maybe that's why Zap's story interests me. Maybe there's hope for me too."

"Could be." She softly agreed.

Thankfully Zevon's phone rang to break the somber tone they were drifting toward. "Hi, Gladys." He okayed, uh huhed, and nodded along until hanging up the phone. He turned to Maggie, "We got quite a bit. I forgot to mention the paddleboat that went down but she found Sally's name in a small promo article about it in the Seattle Times archives. Her name is listed in the cast of several University of Washington productions and in the Philharmonic records but she couldn't find anything with Sally's name in association with John Andrews's productions. There were several articles about him. Gladys is seeing if there are any community paper records. The World's Fair was a boom. Sally's name appears in a program in an international archive and best of all on a promotional flyer about the Joe Vanutti Band but sadly there was only a caricature of him, not her. We are really going to be able to document the story. This is great."

Chapter 10

Hank was a watchmaker and a jeweler, at long last. It took his hard work coupled with Sally's persistence but he now sat shoulder to shoulder with the journeymen in his chosen profession as well as a bevy of apprentices like himself.

It was Hank's interest in his youth with machines and mechanisms which drew him to a dream of watchmaking. He was fascinated with the precision of the inner workings and was blessed with the patience and attention to detail required for the work. Many old watches and discarded clocks were sacrificed to fuel his interest but just as many were resurrected.

When Hank and Sally were still dating they'd once gone for lunch at a quaint teahouse on the peninsula. The small establishment served meals to only ten customers a day on the days they served food at all. It was run by two elderly women revered for the quality of the cuisine. While dining, Hank noticed an antique mantle clock which wasn't running. The clock was built in 1896 by a renowned craftsman. Hank asked the two proprietors if he could try his hand at repairing the classic piece. They agreed and when he returned the clock, which hadn't worked in decades, it kept time like the day it came from the original craftsman's workshop. Hank was proud and the women were extremely grateful. Hank and Sally found out how grateful ten years later when the last of the two women passed away. In her Last Will and Testament the clock was bequeathed to Hank. It was an unexpected tribute from two women he had barely known. The antique timepiece was valued in the thousands, Hank being offered $4000 by a knowledgeable collector in the 1970's which meant, coming from someone who understood the value, it surely was a lowball offer.

Fred Frost was never tempted to use the letter from Sally to fire Hank. Fred was impressed and quickly enamored by Hank's skill, demeanor, and work ethic. Hank also established himself with his peers. There were no complaints about Hank's work. Fred's problem was the union. The bylaws stated there needed to be one journeyman for every ten apprentices in a union shop. Fred was overstaffed and seniority rules said Hank must go. Fred was disappointed. He'd been sufficiently impressed by Hank that he recommended Hank to Frederick and Nelson, a large upscale department store in Seattle. The store hired Hank and again he flourished; within six months he was a member in good standing with the union.

With Hank's steady employment, Sally hit the streets once more, this time to find them a place to live so they could get out of Aunt Anne's spare room. Sally would walk the neighborhood streets lined with Victorian homes looking for vacancy signs or hints the upstairs of any of the huge homes were vacant. If an upper-level appeared to be vacant she'd knock on the door to inquire if it was for rent. Her's was an unorthodox approach but after a mere hundred or so rejections and one success, Hank and Sally had a room.

All of Sally's criteria were met; the landlady was pleasant, there was a hot plate and an ice box in the room. A bathroom was just across the hall, and best of all they could easily afford it.

Hank and Sally were money conscious, especially Hank. They were witnesses to the shortages and struggles of the people during the Great Depression and the War years. Hank took the lessons to heart and never forgot them. He thought through every purchase he ever made, never succumbing to whims or compulsions and making sure Sally followed suit. Hank could squeeze a nickel until Jefferson screamed.

Sally went to work at International Harvester and the couple's financial life was under way. It took them only three months to save enough for a down payment on a home of their own. It was a fixer-upper located next door to a Lutheran church, not that the location was a deciding factor. Their mortgage payment was $75 a month. They rented out an upstairs room for $25 a month but still they owed money to someone which was painful for Hank, even though it was owed to a bank. When Sally convinced him to buy a refrigerator on installment payments from his employer, Frederick and Nelson, it caused Hank to lose sleep until it was paid off.

The floor of their new home was so slanted it was necessary to hold onto items on the kitchen table to prevent them from rolling onto the floor and across the living room. Excessive alcohol consumption was liable to induce vertigo when transiting the downstairs. No matter, the house was a steppingstone to the dream home they'd yet to discover.

The next housing step was a complete disaster in the Lake Meridian neighborhood. They traded the owner of the derelict property for their house on Eleventh Avenue. The man knew he'd taken advantage of the young couple but Hank and Sally saw potential the owner didn't. The home was a mess, so much so, they were forced to take an apartment on Broadway while they labored on their latest investment.

Their efforts were rewarded when the refurbished house sold and they were able to purchase Sally's first dream home. The house was located on 74th Street and came complete with a manicured yard, vaulted ceilings, and jazz plastered walls. It was the perfect place to comfortably begin thinking about starting a family. Hank was pleased, well at least content; the mortgage payment was $90 a month and they were able to rent the basement for $50 a month.

The plan was coming together except for one ominous reminder of the warnings Sally received years earlier from her doctors at the Shriners Hospital in Portland and from her doctor in Kansas City who'd also cautioned her about the danger of her bearing children. Five miscarriages in five years seemed to confirm the warnings.

Sally went to Dr. Bledsoe in Seattle with her dilemma. He was the first medical professional to offer her hope instead of discouragement. He informed Sally her occasional dizzy spells and possibly her inability to get pregnant were related to a vitamin deficiency. She was pushing herself much too hard; her body was run down. A vitamin regime, healthier eating habits, a positive attitude and the hormonal urges of youth combined for a successful pregnancy within a couple of months.

Nine months later a happy, beautiful baby girl was born. They named her Christine. The year was 1950 or '51, depending on whose memory or official agency was relied upon for the statistics. No matter, Hank and Sally, once more, defied the naysayers and the odds. Chris was a delightful addition, so much so that in 1952, Gretchen, another beautiful baby girl was born.

The Heiss family was growing with the addition of the two blonde haired frauleins'. They moved across the Ship Canal Bridge to the Northgate area of Seattle on Pinehurst Street.

All that was needed to complete the family photograph was a baby boy. At the next two-year interval Sally gave birth to their third child, another bouncing baby girl, Heidi. With three blond females in tow, Sally took her traditional two-year break between children before finally giving birth to a male namesake, Henry William. Bill, as he would be known, was to be the last but surprise of surprises, two years later, Katrina arrived without plan.

Sally inquired of Dr. Bledsoe how she might turn off the baby machine they'd awakened. In his calm, assuring manner he informed Sally, "Honey, you have to cross your legs."

The Heiss clan was complete, four beautiful blonde girls and one hopelessly outnumbered boy. North Seattle was their playground. From the thickly wooded forests, the muddy creeks, to the softball field where Sally would toss their sleeping bags and clothes from the car when they were late coming home once again, the Heiss' roamed the city in search of the next adventure. The girls inherited Mom's tomboy behavior and Bill was all boy already.

Raising a family requires a commitment to routine, responsibility, and obligation. Hank and Sally were workers and that's where they could be found for the lion's share of their waking hours. Sally continued singing whenever and wherever the opportunity arose. Hank loved his kids but the emotional needs of a young girl were an area he was ill-equipped to deal with. Many nights after arriving home on the bus from Frederick and Nelson's his kids could find him at the neighborhood tavern. Sally tended bar and ran cocktails at many different establishments in the Seattle area as well as her singing engagements so she was absent many evenings. Even with the hectic schedules, they found time for camping in the family's Volkswagen microbus. Hank was surprisingly patient in teaching their children how to fish. With all involved in his life, he even found time to bird hunt with his German Shorthair dogs, Fritz and Shotzie, and even to play a little ice hockey. The family never missed a weekend opportunity or a holiday event they could spend on the Long Beach Peninsula visiting Hank and Sally's parents. The result was all five of their children carried powerful memories of their grandparents and the Peninsula well into their adult lives. The kids loved playing in the lavish manicured yard of Hank's parent's house on Sandridge road. Hank's mother, Frances, and her first husband were the caretakers of the Schlitz gardens for the Schlitz family in Milwaukee. Frank Heiss passed away suddenly and Francis along with Frank's foreman, Ervin Klemm, assumed the duties. Ervin and Francis would later marry and relocate to Long Beach with their two teenagers, Hank and Trudy. The Klemm's created a landscape behind their home which astounded visitors and was a testament to their amazing abilities to grow, cultivate, and create. The kids loved the yard designed by the gentle giant, Grandpa Klemm, and loving Grandma Klemm.

There were changes afoot at the Christie home front up the road in Nahcotta as well. They moved up the street, buying a home which possessed a downstairs which served as the local post office. Margarite was

108

postmaster for two years until Bill retired to assume the position. He added a small general store which turned out to be his calling. Spinster Aunt Edna moved into an upstairs room adding her unique character to the Christie household. Every night Aunt Edna would retire to her room to 'play cards' until her spirit beverages lulled her to sleep.

The five Heiss children loved Grandpa and Grandma Christie's quaint little store and the playground of Willapa Bay behind the new house, the same bay which had entertained and helped mold the spirit of their mother all those years ago.

The other positive result of introducing their children to the great outdoors was all would cherish the natural world and strive to share the world with their own children. Hank and Sally had always harbored thoughts of the great outdoors but some dreams seem to fall to the wayside. Before their children arrived, Hank and Sally seriously entertained the idea of buying a sailboat and sailing to Alaska where they'd homestead in the vast expanse of America's last frontier. In a twist of irony, years later, their daughter, Heidi, would actually retire onto a sailboat in the Northwest.

Days become weeks, become months, become years. Chris evolved into a capable surrogate mom while Sally was working and singing. Gretchen and Heidi were best friends and proverbial partners in crime. Bill was playmate as well as the annoying younger brother he was expected to be. Katie was a life-size doll for use and abuse by all four of her older siblings for their and their friend's entertainment.

Hank was at a loss when dealing with his daughters, especially when they began displaying the spirit and later the physical endowments of their mother. Sally was attentive but her frantic schedule led her from the home more than she would have liked. Being raised by Marguerite's religious zealousness convinced Sally her own children would benefit from being raised in the Catholic religion which thrilled Hank's mother. The discipline Hank and Sally feared their children were missing due to their parent's absence would hopefully be provided at a parochial school. They both believed their kids would receive a superior education under the tutelage of the church.

Hank and Sally were extremely disappointed with the decision leading to various showdowns with the clergy. Only their three eldest girls would attend. Chris experienced recurring nightmares as a consequence of her treatment at the hands of the priests and nuns.

Second-grader Heidi was so terrified of Sister Ermalita; the nun literally scared the crap out of her.

The education the girls were receiving combined with the emotional turmoil was not worth paying a premium price tag. The girls were transferred to public school.

Public school was a better fit but Sally still wished she had more time to invest in her children. The Parent Teachers Association was continually soliciting Hank and Sally's involvement. Finally Sally squeezed enough time from her work and singing engagements to attend a PTA meeting. She was enthusiastically welcomed by all. The meeting she chose to attend started with a disciplinary hearing involving the actions of a teacher. The teacher was accused of assaulting a student by swatting the student's butt with her hand. The charges against the worried teacher were read and then she was allowed to state her defense. The parents and the accusing child were also present. The child victim fidgeted and glared defiantly at the teacher, enjoying immensely the discomforting situation the youngster had placed the teacher. At the conclusion, the PTA president, who presided over the hearing, asked if there were any questions from the gallery before he passed judgment.

Wanting to make a good first impression by getting involved, Sally raised her hand. The PTA president recognized her to the floor, again thanking her for her attending the meeting.

Sally stood, calmly stating, "I don't understand why you're disciplining this teacher. You should applaud her. The kid sounds like a little asshole. You should give this woman a raise for having the guts to do what his parents should have done."

Sally never made another statement at the PTA. No further invitations arrived in the mail.

Chapter 11

"Just once I wish I had the guts to stand up like Sally and speak my mind." Maggie strolled into the kitchen to get another bottle of wine for Zevon. She said as she returned, "I have no problem doing my job, but if there's an audience I wouldn't say shit if I had a mouth full. Where does it come from?"

Zevon shrugged, "You got me. I can stand in front of my staff and speak with supreme confidence but if any of them ever mounted a serious challenge, I'd wet myself. What a pair we are, Mags. This woman has overcome more obstacles than us and everyone we know, combined, and she does it without questions and never stumbles.

I've got a master's degree and Sally barely got out of high school but I feel like a moron reading about her. The trials I've faced are trivial. I've never faced any adversity of any consequence. I thought God hated me when I lost the election for student body vice president in high school. My parents thought I was a failure when I didn't go to an Ivy League school. My dad was too embarrassed to tell his friends I was going to NYU. I'm a spoiled, pampered, self-centered crybaby."

Maggie smirked as she filled his glass. "It's not an exclusive club, Z. I could have gone to the Ivy League but I thought it might be too hard. Do you realize of the three of us Zap might have been the only one who faced so much as a speed bump in life and that's only because his parents were morons. We all had a free ride. Sally overcame more as an infant than I have in three decades and most of the time I still feel like a victim."

Zevon nodded along in complete agreement. "No shit. I'm so detached most of the time; I'm an observer in my own life. Aside from being a world-class womanizer, my job is my complete identity. End of story."

Maggie reflected before adding, "Maybe that's what Zap saw in Sally, the resolve to face life without questions or qualifications. Look at us. We're both turning a discerning eye on ourselves and we've never met her. So where to now?"

Zevon was happy to turn the attention away from their personal lives. Self-examination wasn't a skill he possessed nor cared to. Meaningless relationships don't lend themselves to deep philosophical introspection. Twelve hour workdays, plentiful alcohol consumption, and naked bimbos don't require explanation, only excuses.

He reviewed the latest chapter. "We should be able to verify Hank's employment at the department store quite easily. His parents should have retrievable records from Milwaukee and Long Beach. We should be able to find Hank's parents immigration documents. Sally's parents were postal employees so they definitely made it onto microfilm. Their children's birth and school records should be easily accessible. I think at the rate we're going we could edit and release Zap's story as a biographical work if we wanted to. I hope he gives us some hints as to what his intentions were. I definitely want to honor his vision, whatever it was."

"Why is it so important to publish?" She asked. "What makes you so sure Zap was writing Sally's story for his own benefit? It's entirely possible he was commissioned to write her story. History says Zap never wrote anything he didn't expect to be paid for."

Zevon deferred, "You might be right but let's make that determination after we've completed the story and the search. If nothing else, I'm thoroughly enjoying the chase and her story. I hope she is still around, we have lots of politicians who deserve to be spit on more than FDR." He dialed Gladys. "It's me. Check a department store, Frederick and Nelson, in Seattle. Hank was a jeweler there. There should be union records of him also.

Sally had five kids, all born in the Seattle area. See if you can find birth records and also school transcripts. Their names were Christine, Gretchen, Heidi, Henry, and Katrina, born in that order at two-year intervals. The three oldest attended a Catholic elementary school for a few years before transferring to public schools. The latest chapter didn't contain many specifics about Sally's work or singing so the search will have to be general. Use your imagination. What's that?" His eyes narrowed, suddenly he brightened. "Excellent. That's great, Gladys. You are the best. Everything we can find is helpful. I'm sorry, we still haven't figured out what the story means or how it relates to Zap but as soon as we do, you'll be the first to know. Thanks, I'll wait for your call." Zevon didn't wait for Maggie's inquiry of Gladys' latest research find. "Gladys found the hospital records of Sally's throat operation and amazingly the scanned chart had a hand written prognosis saying the subject would not resume singing due to excess scar tissue. Isn't that incredible? Apparently Sally neglected reading her medical chart."

Maggie pressed, "You didn't answer my question. Why do you care about publishing the story?"

Zevon wasn't clear in his own mind why it mattered. His response was as much thinking out loud as addressing her question. "Motivation is hard to pin down. It's entirely possible it's driven by my own ego. I think I'm a decent editor. I seem to have the respect of my peers but at the core I'm also a bit of a charlatan. The lion's share of my literary portfolio came directly from Zap's mind. I'll never write a publishable work but Zap surely would have at some time in his life. He was an extraordinary talent. Zap could have written a bestseller about the mating habits of tree squirrels so just the fact he chose this particular story about Sally means he found something profound and unique about her life or her person. We both feel the passion and emotion in only a first draft. I think whether those traits are attributable to him or to her is immaterial. If the final result portrays his vision, the world should share in it. If it's the power of his prose, fantastic. If it's the strength of her character, so much the better. I have never questioned the perceptions of Zap. He could put into words exactly what he saw and he saw what the rest of us miss.

I guess, my answer is ultimately simple and personal. Zap was my friend. My only friend and I want the world to know the one thing I truly know, Zap was special. Something or someone touched him and he's the only man I know who can make us understand how." Zevon's pain filled eyes embraced Maggie, his expression displaying the only sincere emotion she'd ever seen from him. "I'll miss him."

Maggie couldn't speak. She allowed Zevon to accept his grief. It was his moment in time with his only true friend. Zevon and Zap had marched through their lives wise cracking sarcastic about the unknowing minions they encountered. ZZ over-the-top would never be again. Zevon was alone and on his own; a fact he was being forced to accept.

The phones ringtone spared the two college chums further grief. Zevon answered quickly, "Hello. Okay. Okay." He listened closely to the newspaper's star researcher and her latest findings. He closed the phone, turning to Maggie. "Hank worked at Frederick and Nelson until 1960 when he opened his own jewelry store in the Lake City area of Seattle. We have all of the kid's school records as well as medical records. Christine had many; she suffered from severe asthma as well as assorted allergies. Gladys didn't find anything new about Sally. I guess it's time for another chapter."

Chapter 12

It was the 1960's and Seattle was the cultural hub of the Northwest. Scott McKenzie beckoned young people to San Francisco with flowers in their hair, but the young people of Seattle believed they'd already arrived. The social conscience of the country was waking and the Heiss clan was quickly becoming rebellious teenagers. The three eldest girls not only possessed Mom's fearless spirit, they inherited her boy-bait body and all at very young ages.

There was no denying Hank and Sally, meaning primarily Sally, was going to be fighting a multi-fronted war with her free spirited daughters. The times weren't the only thing changing.

Hank's jewelry store was doomed alongside a thousand others by one single invention, the Timex watch. There was no reason to pay a premium price to purchase or repair a quality timepiece when a Japanese built Timex could be purchased for a fraction of the cost and being so cheap, there was no logical reason to repair one. If it quit, throw it away and buy another. Hank hated Timex watches.

He didn't care much more about his next job, mailman. Working at the Post Office was a good job and he did enjoy being out of doors walking around but it wasn't his passion. He was no longer a watchmaker. To give him hope he would one day be able to quit the Postal Service, he and Sally went into partnership with another woman, Betty, buying a tavern in Bothell, Washington. The bar was called Frankie's and Hank hoped it would offer some options. It wasn't to be. Sally and Betty clashed continually, both women possessing diametrically opposed ideas of how a successful tavern should be run. Hank worked to supplement the workload but Betty didn't think his time deserved compensation since he was Sally's husband.

Hank and Sally devised a scheme to dissolve the partnership. They told Betty they wanted to buy her out for $10,000 knowing full well if Betty believed they believed $10,000 was a fair price; she'd try to turn the tables. It worked, Betty offered to buy them out and they readily accepted. Hank and Sally had another idea.

In addition to family vacations to the Long Beach Peninsula, they'd also traveled numerous times to the Lake Tahoe, Northern Nevada area. Hank and Sally were impressed with the small-town atmosphere and seemingly unlimited business opportunities. The big city of Seattle was ripe with activity but also with distractions and enticements for teenage girls. Hank and Sally decided to buy a bar/restaurant in the Nevada capital, Carson City. Finally they'd get to work as the team they'd envisioned when they bought into Frankie's. The real payoff would be the piano bar where Sally would be able to sing every night. What better venue than her own stage, singing only the songs she wanted to sing. For a woman who only wanted to sing; the stage would be perfect.

A parent's vision isn't necessarily shared by teenage girls. The girl's vision was of teenage boys and not cowtown rural Nevada boys. It was 1969 and Seattle's young men were part of the countercultural revolution.

For the two youngest, Bill and Katie, the move was met with excitement. Chris no longer lived at home having married a young rebel she'd met at Ingram High School. Gretchen reacted to the news of the family move by quickly marrying her boyfriend, John, so she wouldn't have to leave her beloved Seattle. Heidi was fifteen years old and to her dismay she was the cutoff point decided upon by her parents. Despite her tear-filled pleas that she be allowed to remain in Seattle to live with best friend Gretchen; Hank and Sally insisted Heidi accompany the family to Carson City.

Hank and Sally didn't worry too much about Chris. Her young husband, Eric, was a product of the times so he possessed a questioning demeanor but he was intelligent, polite, and respectful. Eric was from a solid family, deeply devoted to the LDS church. Eric's parents welcomed Chris into their family and into their faith, with full confidence she wouldn't allow their son to stray far from the fold. Possessing the spirit of her mother, Eric's parent's faith in Chris was well-placed. Eric would always maintain his independent spirit but never relinquished his faith in his Mormon roots.

Gretchen, they worried about. It was no secret, even to her husband John; she'd married only so she wouldn't have to move. The marriage would be as strong as the foundation that it was built upon; it was doomed.

Heidi was another problem. She was under her parent's watchful eye but not by choice. Moving Heidi away from her first love, Gene, was going to prove more difficult than when Sally, seven months pregnant, climbed the cherry tree in the family's backyard to rescue four-year-old Heidi from the upper branches. The move to Carson City motivated Heidi to pout for only the better part of a year and to make matters even worse for lovesick Heidi, boyfriend Gene's love didn't follow her to the backwoods desert of Nevada.

Conversely, Bill flourished in Carson City, eventually starring on the high school baseball team. Katie meanwhile was waiting in the wings for her special version of a wild child. Regardless of their children's reactions the move was, at its core, for Hank and Sally; a fresh start operating their own business, together. Heiss' Hof Brau was born. At last they tied their work days and fortunes to the other person they trusted most. In addition, Sally would no longer be constrained in her singing passions by the whims of others.

The Hof Brau was ideally located in the heart of Carson City. The Carson Nugget, the town's largest casino at the time, was directly across the street and a mere block south lay the sprawling State Capital complex, the State Legislature, The State Courts, and all the associated support buildings of state government. In a short time the small restaurant was serving overflow luncheon crowds. The workday consisted of twelve to sixteen hours but at the end of the long day, it was all theirs.

Heidi was enlisted to work at the family business. The crowds spilled onto the sidewalk many days and at night after the dinner hour, Sally could serenade their patrons.

The community quickly recognized hard-working, honest people. Hank's personable style was an instant hit and Sally soon built a solid reputation for her singing talents. The final piece to the puzzle was the food which was top notch. Hank's meticulous attention to detail extended to the kitchen and coupled with Sally's confident hard work and culinary skills acquired feeding a growing family, they were a dynamic combination. The tone was set, the mold was cast, but Sally always remained Sally. It was difficult to dislike Hank with his unassuming demeanor but Sally's brash style, though entertaining for most, rubbed some more conservative people the wrong way. If someone desired to know what was on her mind they need only listen to her words. Sally rarely offered a mixed message.

Examples of her brand of honesty were many. One evening the Hof Brau was buzzing, the bar was standing room only while others waited on the sidewalk for a table in the restaurant. The waiting time was forty five minutes to be seated for dinner. The recently elected mayor of Carson City appeared with a large entourage in tow. He and his party pressed past the other patrons toward Sally who would surely seat them without delay. She informed the mayor the wait time was forty five minutes.

His smile was condescending, displaying an arrogant manner toward the uninformed woman who didn't recognize the importance of the man standing before her. With ego dripping from his lips, he inquired, "Do you know who I am?"

Sally smiled, nodded, and calmly replied, "Yes, I do. You're the fucking Mayor. The wait is still forty five minutes." He and the entourage waited for a table. The wait was forty five minutes; Sally made certain of it.

Entertainment and good food were the rule; conflict was the exception, especially after Hank and Sally decided to transform the Hof Brau into a final incarnation, Heiss's Steak and Seafood House. A dinner house was a great showcase for their exceptional culinary skills and a wonderful venue for Sally's song styling. Many nights, tears were dabbed from the corners of carefully made-up eyes when Hank ceased work to stare moon eyed at his wife when she sang his favorite song, 'The Wind Beneath My Wings', a song performed for him and only for him.

The double dose of Hank and Sally coupled with superior food was a winning formula. Sally's voice brought many customers back but so did Hank's secret steak sauce which created a following of its own and was sold independently of the restaurant to retain his secret ingredients.

The couple understood quickly another trait they must covet if their business was going to flourish in a government dominated town; discretion. More laws, agreements, and compromises are reached over meals and cocktails than in the official chambers of government. Sally had little trouble ignoring the conversations taking place around her. Government bored her to tears. Hank was also adept at avoiding involvement in the affairs of the lawmakers. Hank's interest in government extended only to how it affected him financially. It didn't matter to him if the amount was a thousand dollars or a penny, what belonged to Hank was his and he defended what was his.

A perfect example of Hank protecting what was Hank's happened one cold wintry Nevada day. There were parking meters on the street outside the restaurant with a single loading zone but the unmetered spot was always full. Normally, Hank parked somewhere unmetered, but on this day he pulled up to a parking spot with a meter. The roads and sidewalks were treacherously covered in ice. As luck would have it, the parking meter was also frozen so Hank could not get a coin into the slot. When he returned there was a parking ticket on his car. Hank was incensed and went to the courthouse to protest. The court told him to just pay the ticket. His government friends concurred; just pay the fine. Hank calmed his outrage at the injustice and agreed to pay the one dollar fine. He appeared at the courthouse with the silver dollar encased in a block of ice. The reaction to Hank's antics was reported in newspapers coast-to-coast.

Instances of conflict with local government were rare. Hank and Sally were good friends with a great many officials, from judges to legislators. They became close enough that Sally was invited to be a guest of a State Senator at a session of the Nevada State Legislature. The opportunity sounded like fun so she accepted. The Speaker of the House, whom Sally knew quite well, called the House to order before asking her to stand and be recognized. She was seated beside the Senator who'd invited her but once she stood a chant began, from those who knew her from Heiss' Steakhouse, to sing a song. Sally never denied an audience.

Sally had recently recorded a cassette; the tape entitled 'Sally Heiss, Naughty and Nice' was composed of her singing some of her favorite bawdy classics, highlighted by the lead track she'd written herself. The cavernous chamber had never before been graced with such a rousing sound nor would it ever again. Singing acappella, Sally performed her number with her trademark power and passion. The song's title, opening line, and chorus were recorded into the official minutes of the Senate of the State of Nevada, 'I Want to be a Madam in a Whorehouse'. There followed a standing ovation. Only Sally.

Chapter 13

"That's great." Zevon couldn't suppress a chuckle. "It's funny, until today I'd never heard of Sally but I have this idea what she might sound like. Remind me to ask Gladys to see if Sally's cassette is still available. I'd love to hear it."

Maggie agreed, "Definitely. I was thinking. Imagine someone, someday reading the minutes of that legislative session. They'd think it was a business proposal not knowing it was a song. Sally sure is a bold woman. I couldn't address a room like that let alone sing to them. Maybe that's part of what Zap saw. We all seem to sabotage our lives instead of simply accepting life as it's offered. We read more into events than what is really there. Obstacles aren't barriers, they're just obstacles. Most of us commiserate about every setback but Sally just looks at it and finds a way around. How elegantly perfect. I have a master's degree in philosophy and she barely got through high school but she sees things more clearly than I ever have. Sally's correct, it's not that difficult to figure out. There aren't a multitude of choices to life. Accept or reject. Everything else is a diversionary tactic."

Zevon was impressed by Maggie's insights. "It's true. It's Achem's Razor. The simplest answer is likely correct.

You know what's struck me the most about Sally? It's not just her determination to achieve, its how she plows headlong at whatever is in front of her without any reservations. Most people need reassurance from everyone around them before they'll commit to a course of action. Sally just does it. There's nothing bold in that, it's simply confidence in herself and her own judgment. Her unapologetic style compels people to follow; she doesn't try to coerce them. And the severity of the obstacles she's faced is off the charts. I mean, who declares they no longer have polio. I can't even wrap my mind around that one. Her voice is another one. The medical professionals say she won't sing again but she loves to sing, so she sings. What the hell is that?"

"I'm with you. The toughest decisions I make in life is paper or plastic." Maggie shared a grin of surrender. "Think about something else, Z. You and I are reacting to Sally from simply reading Zap's first draft. Imagine the impact she must have made on him to inspire the project to begin with. I would never have believed Zap was capable of experiencing an emotional reaction let alone be affected enough to write about it.

130

The Zap I knew was too cynical to write about futility."

Zevon enthusiastically agreed, "Something else I'm getting from the story is hope and I don't think Sally is driven by hope, so it's must be from Zap. A person needs doubt to employ hope. Sally doesn't have doubt but Zap had it in spades. So do I for that matter. So do most of the people I know."

Zevon refilled his wine glass. "Damn, Mags. What's happening here? I don't harbor any desire to examine my life; in fact, the thought scares the hell out of me."

Maggie lifted her glass, "Here, here. I'm four months out of my latest failed relationship. Shining lights on my dark corners is only going to provoke pain and tears. Let's stick with Sally."

Zevon resisted feigning compassion by asking Maggie about her last relationship. His strength was in disrobing and caressing female bodies not there fragile psyches. "Besides the tape Sally made, what else should I ask Gladys for?"

Maggie was relieved to return to Sally's world, "The restaurant for sure. That article about Hank and the dollar in the ice cube would be great. You might as well get the rest of the kids' school records. The two older girls will have marriage licenses. Definitely get a transcript of that legislative session when Sally sang." She mentally replayed the last chapter they'd read.

Zevon added, "How about Frankie's, the bar in Bothell, and as long as we're collecting official records, we could get the property tax docs from the houses they bought. Hopefully Sally sang outside the restaurant so we'll find more promo material. The local paper in Carson City might have a picture of a new business like Heiss's Steakhouse. I still want to see her and him for that matter."

Maggie had a brainstorm. "Wouldn't the military have a picture of Hank? Whoa! What about yearbooks from Illwaco High? There might be pictures of Hank and Sally."

The phone came out. Zevon was pumped. They were hot on the trail of not only photographs but possibly a recording of Sally singing. Zevon laid out the latest request he and Maggie imagined. His enthusiasm was increasing Gladys' excitement over their challenge in resurrecting a paper trail of the life of Zap's mystery woman. Gladys informed Zevon the cork board wall in the research department was totally devoted to

Sally's documented life. Her assistants on the staff of interns were giddy with pleasure every time one of them added a new kernel of information to Zap's final story. Sally Heiss was the latest obsession in the minds of the research department. Young and old, they all wanted to be the first to produce a photo. Gladys laid out only one ground rule. They would follow Zap's timeline story to the letter. The staff was prohibited from Goggling Sally's name or any member of her family. There was no excitement or satisfaction in going to a movie and only watching the final ten minutes and the credits. Gladys knew how to motivate young workers whose daily tasks were normally boring and routine.

Zevon's smile lit up his carefully tanned features. "Gladys has her geeks in overdrive. She's got them following the story with us. Anyone who Googles Sally gets sent home. I love it."

"I'm getting caught up, too. I swore I'd never have anything to do with Zap again and here I am bopping along like a school girl." Maggie shook her head in disbelief. "You know, I should hate Sally not love her. I was married to Zap for four years; we were together for almost eight; why didn't I inspire him? Regardless of how the story turns out, my ego is going to take a beating."

"You got it all wrong, Mags. You inspired Zap; it just wasn't to look at himself. When you were around he was pretty focused on you." Zevon flashed his patented coed disrobing smile.

She wasn't surprised, "Leave it to a pig to arrive at a sexual solution to a philosophical dilemma."

He shrugged, "I am what I am."

Maggie reached over to pick at the leftover Chinese food still spread out at the end of the desk. She leaned back taking a long pull on her glass of water, "So do you have any thoughts or ideas where this story is heading? You've read more of Zap's writing than anyone, hell; you've likely taken credit for more of his writing than anyone."

Zevon displayed a pained expression. "Ow! That might hurt if it wasn't so true. But no, I haven't. Like I said, this is totally new as far as Zap's work traditionally goes. I think that's why I'm struggling so much figuring out whom to attribute the emotional aspects to. I'm used to sarcasm not passion. Zap has thrown me a curve; one of them is tickling my junk but I'm not sure who."

"Do you ever conceive a thought that doesn't originate in your crotch?" She asked.

Zevon's phone rang saving him from having to defend the virtues of the penis generated thought process. "Yo, Gladys. What do you have?" He listened intently for several minutes before thanking her and turning to Maggie. "They're really digging now. Illwaco High School didn't put out yearbooks during World War Two but one of the interns contacted a woman whose father was principal at the time Hank and Sally were there. She's going through her deceased father's old school photos to see what she can find. We're going to get a military photo of Hank but we have to file a 'Freedom of Information Act' form because Hank was an interpreter which falls under the umbrella of military intelligence. Marriage certificates for the two older girls are on the board along with a copy of the business license for Heiss' Steakhouse. The local newspaper in Nevada is the Carson Appeal; they listed the new license but no photo. The minutes from the legislature haven't all been computerized and since we don't have the exact date, Gladys has them checking microfilm for an entire decade. I was afraid to ask her what kind of bullshit story she gave a government employee to get them to do it. I hope it was legal. What else? Oh, yeah, we have the school records for the three youngest kids and Hank and Sally registered a Volkswagen bus with the Department of Motor Vehicles in Nevada."

Maggie inquired, "What about the article on Hank and the silver dollar?"

Zevon nearly leaped from his seat, "Got it! In fact Gladys said they found five references in five different newspapers. No photos though. What else? Frankie's. We have the business license but that's it."

"Nothing on Sally's singing?" Asked Maggie.

"No. Not in that time frame. We're getting closer, though. We'll have Hank soon. We could have the kids through school pictures whenever we want but I want Hank and Sally first. Let's build this family tree from the top down." Zevon grinned. "I can't believe I'm so jazzed about someone I never heard of before today."

Maggie had a somber thought, "Sally is an old woman. Have you given any thought to the idea she may be gone. What if Zap is writing this story posthumously?"

Zevon pondered Maggie's suggestion for a moment. "Don't ask me why, but I don't think so. As sick as this might sound with Zap gone, if Sally is too, we've got a Shakespearean tragedy. That's great production value."

Maggie scrunched her forehead. "Now you're a morbid pig. Let's read."

Chapter 14

Operating a successful bar and restaurant was more than flipping steaks on the grill and serving frosty mugs of beer from a tap. In addition to cooking, serving, and cleaning there were inventories to maintain, liquor distributors, produce orders, meat deliveries, seafood deliveries, dishes and glassware to replace, menus to update, bookkeeping, payroll, business licenses, and health inspectors. The list was daunting and at times overwhelming but on top of their business obligations, Hank and Sally had three kids at home on Northgate Avenue. Heidi worked at the restaurant but still two teenagers and one on the cusp of teendom required more policing than parenting.

Hank, Sally, and their children's lives took many different paths, none boring or similar. Oldest daughter Chris and husband Eric followed Hank and Sally to Carson City. Eric secured a good job reading meters for Southwest Gas and the young couple bought their first home. Chris became pregnant soon after moving so Hank and Sally were going to become grandparents. They were just pleased to have four of their five children nearby.

Heidi never relinquished her disdain of being forced to give up the excitement of her beloved Seattle and first love Gene for a backwoods cow town in the desert. Her rebellion motivated her to misplace her trust and succumb, naïvely to the advances of an older man. He took advantage of Heidi's innocence and her desperate need to belong. Heidi was sixteen years old and terrified of sharing her predicament with her parents but at seven months pregnant her predicament was too apparent to remain concealed. Grandpa and Grandma's brood was growing quickly.

In September of 1971, Eric Junior was born. One month later, premature, the clan grew as Heidi gave birth to Max.

Hank was old school so Heidi had been hurriedly married to the father, Don, before Max was born. Heidi and Don followed Eric and Chris's example, buying a home in Carson City. Eric arranged for Don to work reading meters with him. Little did any of them realize but Don's seduction of Heidi was the most work he was prepared to do. Don would sleep until noon and guess at meter readings. The job and his marriage to Heidi were short lived but Heidi had a purpose in life, Max, who was a big hit with the women at the restaurant in his makeshift crib made inside an empty paper towel box.

Son Bill was that rare combination of good-looking bad boy and jock. He was a rebel with a vicious fastball, talented enough for a tryout with a local minor league baseball team, the Reno Silver Sox. Bill loved baseball but he discovered his real passion was for the cute as a button, curly haired Fran. Hank managed to convince Bill to join the National Guard after high school. The military instilled the maturity Dad hoped but Bill would never outgrow his high school sweetheart, Fran. They were married and settled into a house Bill, now a carpenter, built for them in Dayton, twenty miles east of Carson City. Bill and Fran would never part.

Katie was the baby. She entered the world of teendom in eye opening fashion, much to her parent's chagrin. Katie inherited more of Mom's physique genes than any of her sisters. Katie became Kat and realized early on that her endowments could open any door or any eyes she required. Kat was a swimmer which only added a toned body to the already lethal arsenal she possessed. She would be arm candy for wealthy businessmen, the object of desire for drooling men, and the object of hatred from jealous women.

Gretchen was the one Hank and Sally thought they'd lost. She stayed behind in Seattle and the only time she visited Carson City, Hank and Gretchen engaged in a terrible confrontation on the sidewalk in front of the restaurant. It ended with Gretchen slapping her father, telling him she never wanted to see him again. Sally cried, alone, believing she'd never see Gretchen again.

To the delight of her parents, Gretchen returned two years later after the demise of her foolhardy marriage to high school boyfriend, John. She joined Heidi working in the family business but her judgment in men went from bad to worse. She connected with another John, this one violent, dangerous, and a mother's worst nightmare.

No matter, their family was once again in the fold and the grand child tally would continue to grow.

Eric and Chris were back in Seattle when Gretchen moved to Carson City. They would follow Eric's parents to Boise, Idaho where they raised five children; Eric, Trina, Levi, Mandi, and Hyrum.

Gretchen eventually moved to California, dedicating her life to adoptive children. She was destined not to bear children of her own but she adopted and raised two boys; Kyle and James, as well as the dozens of other children who stayed at her home on their way to new adoptive homes. Gretchen would marry again later in life, but sadly, her husband Doug, passed away after only a few years.

Heidi followed older sister Gretchen's example by following one dysfunctional marriage with another but she would finally meet and marry for love and not need. Heidi and her husband raised Max and his son Clint in Flagstaff, Arizona and Reno, before settling in Bellingham Washington after the boys left the nest.

Bill and Fran never left the house he built. Bill was a carpenter for much of his life before learning to drive a truck when the trades faltered. Bill and Fran raised two children, Willie and Lehia.

Kat would once again become Katie as she aged and she also added to the grandchild scoreboard giving birth to Chad and Henry. Katie lived a rustic life until finally meeting and marrying Trevor later in her life.

After so many years, an empty nest was an adjustment. Hank and Sally had successfully raised their brood, they'd survived their teenagers, and they'd remained completely devoted to each other through it all.

Hank was a product of his time, indoctrinated by parents, peers, the military, and entertainment media to be the model of an American man, strong and silent. He was humble by nature and bighearted within limits. Hank's son, Bill, wasn't entirely foreign to him though the generational differences were a barrier. Hank's daughters were a total mystery. He loved them but their wants, needs, and behavior were beyond his ability to comprehend.

The girls were always Sally's domain which was just as well because as teenagers the girls knew they could steamroll Dad. A mother wants her daughters, and sons, to receive all the benefits she was denied. A mother will share in her children's joy but a child's pain is also a mother's pain. It is one of life's great ironies that a mother's shared burden is rarely recognized by the child for which she carries the burden. A mother lives the trials of her children whether in their presence or in private tears in the darkness of her bedroom.

Margarite loved her two daughters and dedicated her life to forcibly attempting to show them what she believed was the correct way to live. Sally loved her children and attempted to show them the way by example; indomitable spirit and unstoppable determination were their lessons. Their final lesson was personal; enjoy your life and cherish your partner. Hank and Sally's message was clear to anyone who wished to take notice.

It was their time and time stops for no one. Sally's father, Bill, had departed while Hank and Sally still resided in Seattle. Margarite persevered for nearly a decade after her husband's death. It was out of respect for her parents that Sally never questioned nor sought out her birth mother, though, many times she wondered of her own biological roots. Sally always wondered if meeting her mother would answer those nagging questions and doubts. Why was Sally the person she was? Did she have siblings? Did her mother suffer from the same health afflictions as she? Why did her mother put her up for adoption?

Sally didn't dare ask questions aloud while her parents were alive but time, as with life and death, changes all. Hank saw a television program about adoption searches and encouraged Sally to pursue her questions. Sally was experiencing female health complications as well as learning to deal with the onset of diabetes so getting some concrete answers about her biological past could be medically beneficial as well as curing insatiable curiosities.

The woman Sally initially contacted to search for her mother lived locally so Sally went to meet her. The woman took her into a room full of phone books. They searched for the names on Sally's birth certificate but found nothing. The only information Sally knew was her father was supposed to have died near to the time of Sally's birth and her mother was born in Santa Rosa, California. The search for a death certificate for George King was fruitless because no such man ever existed. The initial search for Sally's mother also came up empty.

The pieces began coming together when Sally and the researcher reapplied for a birth certificate for her mother and discovered a belated birth certificate was issued because Madeline Baber was born at home and not in the hospital. The birth certificate was witnessed by Madeleine's mother and her older sister Orpha. Further searches revealed Madeline's married name was Peterson.

Sally wrote a letter to the only address they'd found. It was three weeks before Sally received a response. It was Orpha who received the letter but it was Betty, Madeline's younger sister who called Sally. Betty was six years old when Sally was born. Sally's existence was a revelation to Betty. With the exception of Madeline's older brother, Ed, none of Madeline's siblings knew she'd given birth to Sally in 1928.

Betty was skeptical of Sally and her motives in contacting Madeline after all these years. Madeline's health was faltering and little sister was going to protect her. Betty Spencer was a genetic Sally in many respects. She was a truck driver and had been since 1945, not a usual occupation for a woman before women's liberation began opening doors. Betty was a free-spirited woman who owned a Model A at sixteen years old. Betty bowled and drank beer with the guys six days a week. Betty had two children but it was Madeline who raised little sister's children.

Betty and Sally spoke at length on the telephone. Betty decided she would meet Sally alone to size her up before informing frail Madeline. Betty nearly let the secret out on a trip down the California coast but she managed to hold her tongue. Betty told her sister she had business in Carson City, did Madeline want to ride along? Betty figured she could put Madeline in a motel while she met with Sally. Madeline couldn't reconcile that Betty could have business in Carson City so she persisted in searching for explanations.

Betty finally snapped, saying, "I found your daughter and we're going to meet her."

The reunion took place at Hank and Sally's house on Northgate Avenue. Tears and hugs were the order of the day from the very

145

instant Madeline and Betty stepped from the car. Sally's mother talked like her, walked like her, her mannerisms were eerily similar. It was one of the most intense, emotional moments of Sally's life. Six plus decades of answers was standing in the flesh before her; with answers to the questions which haunted her all these many years. They hugged, they cried, they laughed. They cried some more.

It took Betty to move the reunion, "Let's get inside before all your neighbors think we're lesbians."

Sally had most certainly found her blood family. She remained in monthly contact with her mother, visiting her and Betty numerous times in San Francisco. Sally was able to stay in touch for seven years until Madeline Astor Baber Peterson passed away. It was a wonderful seven years.

Sally embraced the idea she might once again spread her wings and entertain audiences beyond the confines of the piano bar at Heiss' Steakhouse. It wasn't that she hadn't stepped outside the doors of the restaurant on occasion. Sally had thrilled revelers on the classic paddleboat, Tahoe Queen, on the pristine waters of Lake Tahoe. She'd fronted for the Reno Dance Orchestra. Sally's talent was requested for special events such as the Disabled Veterans Convention at the Reno Hilton and the Nevada State Retirees Benefit. Sally was also no stranger to impromptu gigs with local entertainers like her friend, banjoist Red Watson, who'd introduced her to Mickey Finn. More than any specific engagement, it was simply Sally wanted to sing. Sally loved to sing and people loved to hear her.

Hank and Sally made the difficult decision to sell Heiss' Steak and Seafood House where they'd toiled for nearly three decades. The business they built and loved had served the purpose they set for themselves in 1969. Change of something so long ingrained is difficult to embrace but both agreed it was time. All their children, for better or worse, had lives of their own. So move on they did.

The plan was to supplement the monthly income they'd receive from the sale of the restaurant by working part-time and taking extended trips in their newly purchased forty foot Southwind motor home. The perfect employment opportunity presented itself; cooks and bartenders at a whorehouse. The prophecy Sally sang to Nevada's Legislature had come to fruition. Their kids delighted in telling their friends Mom worked in a whorehouse. Chris may have been the exception but only while she was in Temple.

Sally enjoyed the work and the working girls soon adopted her as their surrogate house mom. Sally was no prude but life in a Nevada cathouse came with a steep learning curve. Many of the women who find themselves in the world's oldest profession arrive from dysfunctional families and from many sordid backgrounds. Sally's absence of judgment endeared her to the girls. Sally was bold and bawdy, always with a ready smile, a joke, a song, or a shoulder to cry on but life in a cathouse is not an ordinary 9-to-5 job.

One reality resided in the fact this particular cathouse was on the outskirts of the town Sally and Hank worked for so many years at Heiss's Steakhouse which introduced Sally to many of the local residents. It was only a matter of time before someone she knew entered the whorehouse to sample the local fare. Sally saw him coming up the walk. She knew him quite well but she also knew his wife. The procedure at a house of ill repute begins when the customer rings the doorbell; the madam answers the door, while all the available girls line up for his inspection. The madam escorted the prospective customer into the parlor where nine sensuous, lingerie clad girls stood in a single line. Their attire, makeup, and names are designed to attract prospective clients to their specific attributes or special disciplines. The whorehouse experience is a show, a fantasy production complete with costumes. Sally wore many costumes in her life but the revealing outfits the girls wore were at a new level, even for her.

The girls begin introducing themselves, "I'm Susie", "I'm Candy", "I'm Stormy", "I'm Heather", and so on down the line. No one noticed Sally slipping from the kitchen and standing at the end of the line awaiting her turn to introduce herself to the prospective john. She was sexually attired in a deeply food stained work apron.

When the introductions reached Sally, she stepped forward, demurely saying, "I'm Sally."

It might have been the customer wasn't in the market for a sixty something prostitute in cook's garb, more likely it was because Sally was a friend of he and his wife. There was nowhere to run. Diving through a window was pointless. He employed the time honored male tactic when busted, he begged. He pleaded with Sally not to tell his wife where he'd gone for 'breakfast'. Sally learned her lesson well in her many years of listening to secrets, confessions, and compromises discussed in her presence at the restaurant. She kept her word to him, keeping his confidence until after his death when she finally shared the story, but not with the man's wife. His name was unimportant to the amusing story, anyway.

Hank and Sally successfully made the transformation to semi- retired so they decided to go all the way. They would sell their house on Northgate and become traveling gypsies. They figured they'd have a lengthy transition period while they downsized after forty five years of family and home collections. At their first garage sale to begin thinning out their possessions, a woman who'd long admired their house, asked about the newly placed 'for sale' sign on the front lawn. Sally sold their house at the garage sale.

Hank built a computer workstation and an area for his jewelers craft in the motorhome. Sally had a karaoke machine, advertising banner, a large assortment of taped music, and a closet full of costumes. They were ready for their new lifestyle. They wandered for nearly two years, from the karaoke bars of Brownsville, Texas to fronting for a Dixieland band in Great Falls, Montana. Sally was sharing her passion on the road and only forty years later than she'd envisioned her tour. The road offered opportunities Carson City couldn't. Sally connected for a time with Ragtime Bob Darch, singing with his band and Eubie Blake in Council Bluffs, Iowa at Bill Bailey's Banjo Bar. She hooked up with Ragtime Bob Darch again at the Oak House in Omaha, Nebraska and for a rousing performance at the Edgewood Resort in Alexandria Bay, New York.

Life on the road can become daunting, especially when both of their former lives transpired in the relative luxury of their own home. Viewed on a showroom floor, a motorhome generates exciting visions of exotic destinations brought to you in spacious luxury but in the course of one or two years, the walls begin closing in. Hank and Sally began talking of establishing a home base.

Wanderlust led them to Ajo, Arizona where they purchased a modest home in an adult community. Hank and Sally were officially snowbirds. They'd winter in Ajo and hit the open road for cooler climates in the summer. The open road normally led back to Long Beach.

The Southwind would be parked on the back lawn of the home of Hank's mother where his sister Trudy and her son Warren lived to assist Frances, until her passing. After Trudy and Warren's time in Grandpa and Grandma Klemm's home, Trudy's daughter, Kathleen, and her husband, Mark, would purchase the family home, welcoming all family members to the Long Beach Peninsula for years to come.

Kathleen lived most all her life in Washington State and spent many summers and weekends at Grandma Klemm's house. She and Mark wanted to share her memories with their two daughters, Mallory and Theresa. The Fourth of July would become a family celebration in Long Beach, and Hank, Sally, Mark, and Kathleen would become close friends during those summers together.

We are meant to cherish family because there is one reality which cannot be ignored. Time is not ours to keep; it is borrowed from an eternity where it must be returned. Frank Heiss was gone, Grandma and Grandpa Klemm as well, Bill and Margarite Christie and Madeline Baber had passed on. Much too soon, Trudy's son, Warren, succumbed to a lengthy battle with his health. Kathleen's mother Trudy would follow her beloved son soon after. The trial of life neglects no one.

Fate rides the winds, it rises and falls with the tides, but never does it announce a destination. Hank was diagnosed with cancer on a Tuesday afternoon. Wednesday began a new chapter in their lives. The end of recreation on the open road normally accompanies a diagnosis of civilization's disease. Hank and Sally reacted quite differently; to no one's surprise. They carried on with their life; Sally sang, Hank worked at

152

his hobbies, they traveled, and Hank received treatments wherever they happened to be. Sally would call ahead, carry his medical files, and arranges therapies around their life instead of the other way around.

People who didn't know Hank and Sally would never know they were battling for his life. They traveled, laughed, and socialized like the fun filled couple they'd always been. Hank defied a medical explanation. He maintained his weight and held onto his hair, never relinquishing his joyful, positive attitude. Hank resisted even discussing his disease because there were happier things to talk about. Only Sally knew the painful ravages Hank endured. It was Sally who helped her husband into bed after the powerful, invasive treatments sapped every ounce of his strength. With the same resolve Sally employed in her life; she honored Hank's strength by never allowing her smile to fade. Sally stood like the towering giant she'd always been, beside the man she loved. Her tears fell in the darkness, alone. Sally's pain would have to wait. Together they willed Hank into remission.

Chapter 15

"I'm not sure I like where this is heading," said Maggie. Her emotions lay closer to an invisible precipice than she cared to acknowledge. There was a raw honesty simmering just below the surface. "I don't want your Shakespearean tragedy but on the flipside I don't know how inadequate I'd feel if Hank and Sally defy mortality. I'm not that strong. I start writing my obituary when I have a bad case of the flu."

Zevon grinned at her vulnerable honesty. "Me too. The story though, is about life and we're documenting it. It's a real life and life has a beginning and an ending. I think as far as our research, we've come to a crossroad. We could branch out by following all of the children's lives but I'm not sure if that's helpful or pertinent to our interest in Sally's life. What do you think?"

"I agree," replied Maggie. "We should draw a line and say that's all we need, like marriage licenses, grandkid's birth certificates and maybe their location. Beyond that it starts becoming a story about the kids. Maybe that will be necessary later but I don't believe it is right now."

Zevon nodded, "Agreed. Let's only include anything that pertains to interactions between Hank or Sally and the kids. Other than that we've got some awesome new information. We've got singing engagements." He paused for a chuckle. "I can't wait to tell Gladys about the whorehouse. I wonder what kind of public records they are required to file? Then there's the morbid stuff, Hank's medical records for his cancer treatments."

Maggie added, "Don't forget the material from her biological mother and her family. There's a lot there and that's important to the story. I was wondering if we should get more on Sally's adoptive parents also."

Zevon had resorted to taking notes for reminders of the items he needed to relay to Gladys. "Anything else?"

Maggie shook her head. Zevon pulled the phone from his pocket, "Gladys, are you ready for this. I've got a lot." He relayed everything he and Maggie agreed upon and then listened closely for an extended time. He turned to Maggie as soon as he closed his phone. "We're going to lose some researchers real soon. They're going to be on overtime and Gladys can't authorize overtime pay and neither can I. She did get the article on the paddleboat sinking on Lake Union but the lady in Illwaco still hasn't notified Gladys about any pictures. DOD records will e-mail

Hank's military photo before close of business today."

An uncomfortable silence fell between them. Maggie and Zevon stood on a crossroad of their own. They were faced with the choice of discussing the story of Hank and Sally or forging deeper into reflection of their own lives which Zap's story had inspired. The problem was neither Maggie nor Zevon were comfortable casting a critical eye on themselves. All they had in common was tied to the untimely demise of their friend whose only commonality lay in the past. It was a condemned bridge spanning yesterday to the present and neither Maggie nor Zevon knew how to begin crossing the divide.

Zevon led them to safe ground. "What may prove interesting is if it's the trials of Hank's health that sparked Zap's interest. Tragedy has a way of defining our lives and how we react dictates who we will be going forward."

"Zap never talked about his family, in fact, I never met his parents. Was there some illness in his past that might have caused him to find some parallels with Hank and Sally?" Maggie hoped she didn't appear bitter her husband hadn't shared his background with her.

Zevon didn't pick up on any latent emotional tones. Reading women was not in his skill set. Recognizing distress in a woman was quite foreign to him, he was usually the source of a woman's distress. "I knew Zap's parents but only in passing. I don't think I ever had a conversation with either one of them. Zap treated them with the same indifference he treated everyone. If they were ever sick, he didn't say anything to me. It's sad, but I have no idea if they're even alive. If that's Zap's connection to the story, I have no idea where it comes from. Now that you mentioned it, it's kind of strange Vince contacted you and me to go through Zap's stuff and not his parents. I didn't think to ask him."

Maggie commented, "It was only a thought. I'm sure Vince merely wanted to make sure there was nothing incriminating in the apartment. He knows how close you and Zap are so I'm certain he just wanted you to protect Zap's intellectual properties which, I guess, is what we're doing. I don't know if Vince would guess we'd be developing them, too."

"I thought about looking around for Zap's notes or interview tapes but I'm afraid I'd get ahead of the story and, honestly, I don't want to ruin it. For me it has a parallel significance. I'm profoundly impressed by the way Sally has conducted her life but in the same respect I'm Zap's biggest literary fan so I'm immensely enjoying his take and treatment of her story. Emotional content is so new coming from Zap but he's never attempted any genre that he didn't excel at. That will be the saddest part of this. Even if we develop the story, no one will be able to duplicate what Zap himself could have done with it. No one." Zevon's words ended with genuine sadness. Zap's written words were a final truth to his best friend.

Gladys seemed to know when Maggie and Zevon needed to be rescued from themselves. Despair was only a teardrop away.

Zevon answered the phone. He picked up a pen, taking notes as he nodded, okayed, and uh huhed along with Gladys' information. At several points he chuckled and exclaimed, "Really, that's great."

Maggie anxiously waited. Zevon hung up the phone and turned with a smile. "You won't believe it. Gladys' entire staff clocked out but they're all still helping out. Everyone wants to know the story. Anyway, the whorehouse stuff is awesome. They went at it through the tax records. Prostitution is legal in Nevada so everything is above board. They even have Sally's signature on an inspection form from the health department. And get this, Sally didn't work at one whorehouse, she worked at three. She is listed as cook and runner, whatever that is, at Kittie's and at the Moonlight Ranch. The Moonlight records say Sally was terminated. They're trying to find someone who can elaborate on that. The Moonlight Ranch is still in operation with the same owners. Sally also tended bar at the Sagebrush Ranch on weekends." Zevon was excited to giddiness, "That is so cool.

The Tahoe Queen went bankrupt but there are promotional flyers at several museums. They're looking for Sally's name on any of them. Ragtime Bob Darch was the only name on any of his promotional stuff. But guess what? We have a picture from the Carson Appeal that shows Heiss's Steakhouse. It was in an article about road improvements in downtown Carson City. And we got it, Mags, Hank's military photo. Gladys said the kids don't get it but she's old enough to know and Gladys says he's movie star handsome and real young.

There's a great possibility for Sally from the Edgewood resort in New York. They might still have surveillance video from when Sally performed with Bob Darch. We might be able to get actual footage of her performing in full costume." Zevon was nearly breathless.

Maggie grinned along with Zevon's excited dissertation until a grim reality it her. "What about Hank?"

The thrill drained quickly from Zevon's face, "Yeah that was real. We've got the medical records."

Chapter 16

Phoenix is in the Valley of the Sun but for six months of the year the metropolitan area closely resembled hell on earth. The long drive from Ajo to the cancer treatment center in blistering heat was beginning to take a toll on both Hank and Sally.

As always, instead of resigning themselves to a situation they decided to adapt by selling their home in Ajo and buying a comfortable modular home in Lake Havasu. Hank would be closer to the treatment center and there was an added bonus of great interest to Sally. Sally would have the support of a lifelong friend who happened to live in Lake Havasu. Sally and Winona met many years before in Seattle; a meeting that was arranged to couple Sally's vocals with Winona's piano styling. The two women met, bonded and never released their connection. During the most trying times of Sally's life there was comfort knowing Winona was nearby.

Determination cannot defeat flesh. Spirit bold falls short in the presence of mortal reality. The wonder which was Hank and Sally Heiss was in peril. Together they'd completed many journeys in fifty seven years of marriage. Every goal they'd set for themselves was achieved. They'd witnessed their family grow and prosper. All of their lives, in work and play, spent in the constant presence of one another. True love needs not be spoken, only shared. Respect is a condition not requiring acknowledgment.

Sally had boldly charged through every roadblock, obstacle, disease, doubter, and illness with unwavering faith. The coming day was always her pursuit but biology was an opponent she was impotent to face down; there was a foe she could not conquer. Her sobs wracked only herself as she saw pain in the eyes of the strongest man she'd ever known. Sally's tears fell in silence. She would not bear her pain before her beloved.

Hank wanted to see home, Long Beach, where he and Sally fell in love; where they defied the doubters while planning and building a life together. Sally drove the Southwind to Long Beach, parking it on the grass of the home where he lived when he and Sally first met. Hank knew his days were near but none who came to see him would believe that truth.

As with life, Hank and Sally made decisions with one heart. He was taken to a hospice in Portland, Oregon where compassion ruled political correctness and dignity was a decision for loved ones, not legislators.

Four of Hank and Sally's children were able to extract themselves from their busy lives to be in the presence, one final time, of their father. To a person they were amazed this great man could be gravely ill. How? His smile was strong and genuine; he joked with his children. He even lobbied for a sponge bath from an attractive nurse.

Sally was more than just Sally, she was Hank's Sally; the woman who'd been his tower of strength, his beacon of light through the darkness. She summoned all her power to assure Hank all would be all right even as a vice slowly crushed her heart. Sally swore the final sight; Hank's eternal vision would be his adoring soul mate's smiling face.

There is a power unknown in normal lives; it resides only in precious few. Sally searched, found, and subdued that very strength from somewhere. The hospice nurse empowered Sally with control of the morphine drip which was relieving Hank's crushing pain. Her other hand held his while she sang to her beloved. There exists but two people who have ever lived who know whether Hank began his final journey of his own accord or with the helping hand of his loving wife and it doesn't matter. There was no agony; only love, respect, and dignity. Hank's eyes closed one final time to the loving vision of his adoring wife's smiling face.

To be mortal is to have a finish line, no exceptions. Hank's ashes were set free to the winds, in the presence of those who loved him, at Beards Hollow beneath the towering cliffs standing sentry over the mystery of the vast blue Pacific Ocean. On those winds he'll ride until a day when Sally joins him.

Loss alters time. It is true; nothing will ever be the same. In the time of a heartbeat, a chapter ends. Only true giants rise again. Sally was experiencing tragic new depths in emotions, before unknown; stirred from new corners, never before reached, assaulting her being. Sorrow, loneliness, loss, self-pity, and one terrifying new emotion; fear.

There are but two solutions to fear and they are burned into our primal, instinctual, core self. Fight or flight. There are no other answers. Flight was so foreign to Sally as to be no choice at all. She employed a tool she'd possessed since her very first breath, all those years ago in San Francisco; Sally accepted. She accepted her pain because it could never have existed without her love. She'd offered every ounce of herself to another and him to her. Their gift of love, given to themselves, is life's only blessing.

There were no therapist's couches for Sally to help her discover a new tomorrow. Death cannot be defeated; only in life can it be accepted. Sally embraced her life. She remembered only the joy she shared. Sally released the piece of heart she'd shared with Hank. She released him like she'd lived her entire life; with a smile on her face and a song in her heart. Sally picked up her pen to write another chapter.

Chapter 17

Maggie was much too close to the edge to stop. The tears came unabated. "Dammit!" She declared, hurrying into the kitchen for a paper towel.

Zevon said nothing, silently slipping away to the bathroom. His emotional response would be kept to himself. Men don't cry, at least in the presence of a witness.

They had their Shakespearean tragedy and even though it came as no surprise, neither Maggie nor Zevon was capable of controlling their reaction to the reality revealed in Zap's story.

Both were back in control of their outward emotions when they returned to the computer desk. Maggie refilled Zevon's wineglass as well as her own while Zevon watched blank eyed, hoping she would steer the conversation. Mortality was another of life's subjects he was clueless of conjuring a verbal, let alone a compassionate reaction.

Maggie held up her glass for a toast. "Let's have a drink for Hank. I never met him but I feel like I'm going to miss him." They gently touched glasses before offering Hank's toast to their lips. Maggie said, "I want Zap to write my life. He was worthless at helping me to live it but I love the way he writes it. Fifty seven years. That's incredible. I don't know anyone who's been together that long and Hank and Sally did most of the time in each other's face. They went out of their way to be together. I'm speechless."

Zevon, the uncrowned king of noncommittal relationships, was equally impressed. "You know what really got to me? As sad and tragic as that was, the chapter ended with a message of hope. How is that possible? Was it how Zap worded it or was it Sally's spirit? I'm being drawn in different directions but there's no denying the message."

Maggie grinned. "There's no conflicting message, Z. There are no distinctions to be made. It's not a matter of his or hers, there's simply hope. Trying to pin down the origin is pointless, hope exists. It's there because strength willed it present. Hope is undeniable exactly because of that strength. It's hard for you and me because we relinquished our grip on hope long ago. Maybe there's hope for us yet."

Zevon lifted his glass again, "Maybe you're right. I certainly don't have an eye on the future. I haven't made plans for the weekend.

You want to hear a really strange one? Sometimes while we're reading the story, I feel like Zap's trying to say something to me, personally. I can see a change and a growth in his words and it's like he wants me to see what he sees. Is that too bizarre?"

"On the contrary," Maggie replied. "It sounds to me like you've experienced a maturity moment. No wonder it's confusing to you. Zap wrote me a letter because he needed to plainly say what he wanted me to know but he had to know you were going to eventually read this. Maybe not his first draft but you are his editor and his best friend. If Zap experienced some sort of epiphany, of course, he'd want to share with you.

I know exactly how you feel about the story. At times, I think Sally is staring at me, saying 'are you paying attention?' She is so real. I'm a scared little rich girl living behind a mask. I give them what they expect. In our world, we meet someone and instantly catalogue and categorize them. Where do you work? Where do you live? Who do you know? None of it's real. It's all part of the illusion. We become the picture on our Christmas cards.

Sally tells me to seek out who I am. Discover who I want to be. Don't live for other's expectations. Find yourself and embrace you. I'm humiliated and hopeful in the same breath."

Zevon shook his head. "I'm not sure I'm up to the challenge. My solution to self-realization is copious amounts of alcohol and naked woman. Maybe I'm not really shallow at all. Maybe I simply reached my potential already."

Maggie laughed, "Right, Z. You didn't believe it while you were saying it but I'll let you off the hook. What do you need from Gladys with this latest chapter?"

Relief flooded Zevon's carefully appointed features. Professional confidence took over, even his posture inflated. "This one's a little tougher. We might have trouble hanging onto our unpaid research staff with the tone of this one. I'd say we could e-mail them the chapter but I don't want anyone to see any excerpts until we've decided what we've got." He looked inquisitively at Maggie. "What do we have? Any ideas? I mean, this story isn't going to go on forever. Sally has to be pushing eighty and for the life of me; I can't decide whether this is a biography or a novel?"

Maggie shrugged, "What if Zap didn't know either. He did just blurt things out for all his first drafts. What if he was going to simply put it down before stepping back to see what he had? And for that matter, what difference would it make? It's a story. A story about the real life of an extraordinary woman. We're documenting her life, so we know it's real but, ultimately, does that make it any better? Would the story of Sally's life touch you, me, or prospective readers any less if it weren't true? I don't think so. Zap identified some intangible quality which might or might not exist but it profoundly moved him to attempt to share it. That's a message worth sharing in any genre."

Zevon reflected on Maggie's words long and hard before replying. "How did you get so smart? So I guess all we need from Gladys is the records from the hospice in Portland and I'd like to see a picture of Beards Hollow. That should be easy enough to find. Anything else, Mags?"

"No, I guess not," Maggie replied. "Everything else I want, I need to extract from someone's thoughts." Maggie chuckled with a thought to help her diffuse the dark mood they'd created. "Let me qualify that remark. Someone's thoughts other than yours. I know yours always begin and end X rated."

Zevon pulled out his phone, "Truer words were never spoken. Gladys, how are we doing?" He listened, nodding slowly. Suddenly his eyes opened wide, he turned to Maggie while still listening. "That's awesome, Gladys. Well, we don't have too much from this last chapter. Hank passed away at a hospice in Portland Oregon in 2003. I'd like to get a photograph of a place called Beards Hollow on the Long Beach Peninsula. And I can't wait, send what you found to my phone. Thanks, Gladys. I'll get back to you real soon. I don't think we have too much farther to go."

Zevon hung up but held onto his phone. His grin was devious as he turned to Maggie. "We got it, Mag's. Remember the woman in Illwaco who was looking for high school pictures of Hank and Sally in her father's things? Well a friend of hers knew Hank and she e-mailed Gladys a picture of both of them, Hank and Sally, on the beach together. Sally is seventeen and Hank is twenty or twenty one. It was before they went to Kansas City." Zevon smiled as if they'd found the Ark of the Covenant. "We did it, Mag's. Are you ready to see them?"

Maggie nodded, "Yes. I feel like we've been searching forever but we only met them today."

Zevon's phone rang, announcing the message was being received. He slid his chair beside Maggie so they could view the couple together. The tiny screen on Zevon's phone didn't offer much but Hank and Sally were there. Hank was smiling broadly through his classically chiseled features. He wore slacks and a button-down, short sleeve shirt. His arm was proudly placed on Sally's shoulder. Her smile matched his; young love and unlimited possibilities shone from their eyes.

Maggie pushed closer to better see Sally. Her pants were rolled up to mid-calf. The sleeves on Sally's shirt were rolled up onto her upper arms. The loose hanging shirt was helpless to conceal the voluptuous body beneath. But it was the face, the eyes Maggie strained to see. It was as if Maggie believed Sally would be there with a personal message. There was joy in Sally's expression but there was another quality so many people lacked; certainty. Sally claimed her place in the world. "Do you think Sally knew that night at the dance at the Siberian? She was a freshman and Hank was a senior. Do you think she really knew?" It wasn't truly a question.

Chapter 18

Life is a series of tragedies punctuated by choice. The tragedy exists only for those left behind but that also is a choice. Mortality presents only a crossroad, not a roadblock. To stop is but another choice. To resist inevitable change is futile. We must face forward to view future horizons. Miring ourselves in only the pain of the past is a misplaced tribute to those we've lost. Some people need direction to new paths, some simply know.

Sally always knew her way. Fond memories couldn't remove pain but they told her how worthy her trial had been. She drew strength from all she and Hank were in life; she stood tall to better see life's road ahead.

Leaving Long Beach was a testament to strength of purpose. This was where they'd begun and driving away without Hank beside her seemed as foreign as waking without seeing his face. Long Beach, the Peninsula, was also where Sally conducted and formulated her own life. Nahcotta is where she'd faced down the bullies tormenting her older sister, Sally swinging a beanpole to prevent the boys from disrobing hapless Mary Jane. Nahcotta was where Sally shot a black bear in the butt and crawled through the mud stalking a goose for dinner only to put four bullets into a decoy. Nahcotta was where her beloved father lived out his days, happier than he'd ever been, running a general store. It was where Sally's mother hopelessly attempted to control her headstrong daughter's spirit. Everything eventually changes.

Eric and Chris drove to Long Beach to assist Sally with driving her vehicles home to Lake Havasu. The motorhome needed only to go to California where Gretchen's partner, Bill, purchased the RV as a kindness to Sally. She bore no illusions that the big Southwind was more than she cared to drag about the country.

Once home, family and friends surrounded her with condolences and support but all had lives and responsibilities of their own and soon Sally found herself alone. It wasn't solitude which had her staring at the ceiling at night, it was the finality. There were also real world consequences she could not deny.

Her home in Lake Havasu was owned, free and clear, but her income was a paltry social security check and installment payments from the sale of the restaurant. Austerity was the new reality. Hank's financial training was going to come in handy.

More so than her financial situation, Sally's biggest problem was the idle time. She renewed memberships at the Eagles Lodge and the VFW where karaoke was a mainstay. Sally knew activity would be the key to future happiness. Thankfully, Winona lived nearby but she also had a life of her own to conduct. It wasn't like someone being beside you for conversation or assurance late at night. A majestic Arizona sunset is all the more majestic when there's someone with which to share.

Sally's business card contained a color picture of her smiling face. She wore make up for the stage; flashy long crystal earrings, a sparkling necklace around her neck, a black feather boa, and a long plumed feather hat on top of her silver curls. The text declared "Frivolous Sal", entertaining vocalist for all occasions. Jazz, Blues, Broadway, and Country. Sally Heiss.

Her closet was filled with sequined gowns she'd sewn for many engagements through the years. There were wigs, boas, costumes, masks, heels, and drawers of costume jewelry. Sally was ready for any eventuality. One thing hadn't changed nor would it ever; 'Frivolous Sal' could still sing. The only change would be her most devoted fan would not be seated in the front row; he'd relocated to the warmth of memory. Sally was a regular on karaoke night in Lake Havasu. When she took the stage, all else fell away.

The eyes glistened in the lights, failing legs swayed her aging body, and the voice of her entire being filled the air for all those blessed to hear.

Sally's children and their families lived far away. They visited when they could but weekends and occasional vacations were not sufficient to be part of daily life. Eric and Chris, along with Eric's brother Kirk and wife Cheryl, invited Sally along on an extended road trip in Eric and Chris's motorhome. She had a wonderful time but as with every other day, at the end of a vacation or a visit, Sally went home to be alone.

She dated, for a time, a pleasant man she'd known from the Lodge. It wasn't a romance but at least it was companionship. Sally was dating him when she went to her doctor for a routine visit. She told the doctor her heart, at times, felt like it skipped a beat. He told her it was likely nothing but sent her for further tests, nonetheless. Sally received a triple bypass operation that very day. The man she was dating never called again. Eric and Chris were there for Sally's recovery for two weeks after her surgery, followed by Gretchen for another two weeks but, all too soon, Sally was once again alone.

Money is a man-made evil and curse but the necessity cannot be denied. Sally was persevering until the payments from the restaurant suddenly ceased. The buyers defaulted on the loan and Heiss's Steakhouse faded away, becoming only an unlit yellow neon sign.

Sally was in trouble. The check she received from Social Security was totally inadequate to support her. She figured her savings were adequate to sustain her for two years. Her problem arose from the fact she intended to live much longer than two years after she'd outgrown the effects of old age. Sally started informing her family and friends she would die in two years; that was how long she believed her savings would last.

Humor and spirit can't replace reality. If a new chapter were to be written, Sally would need to write it. What she wrote was a personal ad and she placed the ad in a Yuma, Arizona newspaper; Yuma being the widow and widower capital of the Southwest desert. Sally's predicament wasn't desperate, yet, but it would be. Her only other option would be to move in with one of her daughters but she had no desire to become a burden when she was quite capable of taking care of herself. She needed a partner.

There were two responses to her ad. The first was slightly bizarre and totally confusing. The response came from a twenty one year old African American man who was soon to begin a lengthy prison sentence. He professed his fetish for older woman and desired a pen pal and a place to stay on his release. Sally figured he would either rob her or confuse her and he'd already accomplished the latter. He was much too young to realize he was overmatched.

Sally received a phone call from a polite, pleasant man who was of similar age to her. They conversed for a long time discovering many areas of common interest and experience. He said he would like to drive to Lake Havasu to meet her in two days if that were agreeable to Sally. She concurred and hung up the phone. He must have replayed the conversation in his head and liked what he heard because he called again within a few minutes inquiring if he could come see her the following day.

Conflicting thoughts wrestled in Sally's mind. Was this a mistake? At her age, was she too set in her ways and he in his to forge a relationship? No matter. He was coming the following day from Yuma.

Whether in your teens, forties, or seventies, blind dates come with nerves. When a new Saturn sedan pulled into the driveway and stopped, it was too late to go back. With schoolgirl anticipation, she watched a neatly dressed, white-haired tank of a man emerge from the Saturn. He was slightly shorter than Sally but it could be only perception due to his powerful build. Broad shoulders, a barrel chest, and thick arms told the tale of a man who labored at physical jobs for all his life. He moved very deliberately, another testament to a life of strenuous work. Leading the man to the door was his canine alter ego. Sporting auburn hair; a rotund, short legged Corgie waddled toward Sally as if they'd been separated forever. Goldie's little legs barely kept her well fed stomach from dragging the ground. Her gentle eyes and wagging tail greeted Sally like an old friend. Goldie climbed into Sally's lap.

The man who returned Sally's long lost friend, whom she'd never met, followed Goldie into the house. His name was Arvon Edward Pfeifle, Ed, and his pale blue eyes were as gentle and caring as his canine companion. As coincidence would have it, Ed was of German roots. He was polite, gracious, and exceedingly respectful. The most enduring and apparent quality Ed possessed was a huge heart which he humbly wore on his sleeve.

Sally spent her life around customers, fans, family, and business associates. Judging character was a skill she possessed in spades and rarely would she be proven wrong. Beside the fact or possibility in addition to the fact, Ed was as cute as Goldie. Sally saw one other quality which couldn't be concealed; Ed Pfeifle was a good man. His body bore wounds from the Korean War and decades of hard toil but his humble manner was hard to resist. Besides, he'd brought Goldie home.

Sally's assessment of Ed's character was affirmed when he told her he'd stopped drinking and smoking, at the same time, thirty years earlier and never relapsed. Addiction rules many lives but Ed saw the peril in his life and simply stopped after years of abuse. Though Ed endured torture and tragedy in his life, his ready smile and infectious laugh belied his painful past. A man shoulders responsibility without complaint or reservation. There was no doubt Sally was in the presence of a man.

Ed and Sally were two separate pieces to the same puzzle. Sally owned a home and Ed drew a healthy collection of monthly checks. The material and financial aspects of their lives couldn't have meshed more perfectly. The speed with which they personally meshed was the icing on the cake and within a short while it became a wedding cake. Ed and Sally didn't actually have a choice, Goldie was home.

There is no template for love, no two the same. Ed and Sally created their own; not built of youthful exuberance but of mature respect, not of insatiable need but a mutual desire for companionship. Love does not conform to preconceived notions; it embraces those with the courage to accept. A new chapter began for both, together, as all great unions are forged.

Sally offered another benefit long lacking in Ed's life; family, lots and lots of family. Five kids, thirteen grandkids, and twenty two great grandkids. There were times the sheer numbers would be overwhelming to a man so accustomed to solitude. Ed in turn offered Sally a unique opportunity; one she'd never experienced. He encouraged her to spend money.

Ed was generous to a fault and his appointed task in life was to make sure his new bride possessed everything she desired. Sally could mention in passing something she thought attractive and it would appear. Money meant nothing to Ed but Sally meant everything. One day Ed witnessed her struggling to reach up to close the hatch on the car and before she could say brand new Chrysler Town & Country Van, they owned one. Power doors, windows, seats, Sirius satellite radio, GPS, TV monitors, the Chrysler did everything but the shopping.

When it came to money, Sally's two husbands were different as night and day. Fifty seven years of miser training was a daunting task to overcome but Ed was the man for the job. Spending money with Hank required pleas and carefully planned manipulation; spending money with Ed required pointing. Her two husbands were different as could be but shared what was most precious, Sally loved them both. Two spectacular sunsets are never the same but share in their magnificence. Paths cross at different times in life and sometimes it simply works because the time is right.

Ed and Sally shared another trait which couldn't help but endear them to one another. Ed possessed a powerful, operatic voice. Though he'd never developed his talent he recognized Sally's; whether singing karaoke at the Lodge or at a community production at the Havasu Civic Center, Ed was Sally's raucous cheering section and vocal press agent. Ed's rambunctious ovations could at times border on embarrassing and 'Frivolous Sal' was not easily embarrassed. Ed's ear heard a sound from the heavens and he didn't apologize that he believed the world should know it.

It wasn't only husbandly prejudice. The worst place for a name to be on the list of those waiting to perform at karaoke was behind Sally. After Sally performed a number, would be singers suddenly recalled prior engagements, or experienced sudden health problems. An echoing voice while alone in the shower doesn't always translate to an entertaining stage voice. Some should remain soaped up in their bathrooms. Then there is Sally. She holds a karaoke microphone because that is the venue open to her. Sally sings because she loves to sing. Sally never picked up a microphone in the hope of fame or fortune but only to share, to entertain. Passion is personal. Passion is not a skill to be taught or rehearsed. Passion grows from a deeply rooted place born of intangible desire. Sally would sing before an invisible band, surrounded by an imagined production set, always with an indescribable energy, drawing her audience along on the entertainment journey she rode with every ounce of her strength, every time she sang.

Sally would surprise even family when she possessed a stage. On vacation with Eric, Chris, Kirk, and Cheryl she converted another skeptic. Kirk had never heard Sally sing so when he witnessed her frail body struggle to mount the stairs of the stage at a karaoke club in Tennessee, he was justifiably concerned. He hoped Sally retained enough strength she wouldn't embarrass herself and in the process, them. When Sally's booming voice stopped reverberating in the barroom, to a standing ovation, Kirk's apprehension was converted to that of another adoring fan.

Ed and Sally continued traveling in his forty foot Winnebago but father time was creeping up on both of them. Sally's determination was finding old age a worthy adversary. There was a possibility she might have to revise her strategy of outgrowing old age. There may be a flaw in her theory.

Sally decided to replace the worn out parts starting with a hip replacement. Ed and Sally were realistic about their ability to man handle her during rehabilitation so she was transferred to a nursing home after surgery. Surgeons replaced her hip but her attitude was never in need of repair. Sally had endured diabetes for many years so she required a blood sugar test daily. When the orderly entered the room to conduct the test, she dutifully held up her finger of choice for testing. The first day the orderly was stunned by Sally's smiling one finger road rage salute but soon he understood it was just Sally. The young male orderly understood completely when he was giving her a sponge bath. Sally told him to pay close attention because some day his wife would look like her. She said perky breasts at twenty become forty four longs at eighty.

Sally required assistance to get out of bed for trips to the restroom. Her bladder didn't seem to care if the nurses weren't answering the buzzer. Sally was always self-sufficient so she decided she'd simply move her body an inch at a time until she was out of bed. In incremental moves she rolled onto her stomach; phase one. Problems arose when her new hip didn't allow her to put her feet on the floor. Her hands couldn't reach the wall, the bedrail, or anything to help her, and rolling to her stomach was easier to achieve than rolling back. Sally was a stuck turtle, only she was on her stomach. She was stuck, hopelessly stuck.

This would be the time when there would usually be screams of anger and frustration followed by tirades aimed at an inattentive staff. When the orderlies arrived Sally was lost in hysterical laughter at the absurdity of her situation.

Back at home, late one night, the phone rang. It was one of her many grandchildren. They had tuned the television to an HBO special about a Nevada Whorehouse. The song accompanying the open credit was Sally's 'I Want to be a Madam in a Whorehouse', which Sally had performed for the camera in the whorehouse.

It came as no surprise when Sally

Chapter 19

Maggie and Zevon were staring at the blank screen. The story stopped midsentence.

Zevon scrolled forward. Nothing. "What the hell happened? He just stopped." Zevon pushed the mouse away like it had bitten his hand. "You don't think? Zap wasn't writing this when?" He couldn't finish the sentence.

Maggie couldn't tear her gaze from the blank screen. Was that it? Were they destined to never know the ending to the story? Was Zap's enlightenment to go to the grave with him?

Zevon and Maggie turned slowly to face each other, neither could voice their disbelief. Zap had offered his two friends a glimpse of existence beyond their narrow field of vision and suddenly stopped before revealing what it all meant. The story was a revelation tease. They could share only disbelief.

As if a switch were flipped, a grin slowly began to spread across Zevon's lips. Maggie watched, fascinated at his slow but total transformation.

"What is it, Z? What are you doing?" Her grin followed in slow progression along with his.

Zevon said softly, "I'll tell you what I'm doing. I'm going to Arizona. If Sally is there, I'm going to finish Zap's story and then I'm going to ask Sally what she wants done with it. I want to tell her what she meant to Zap." Zevon paused, displaying a confidence never shown before. "What she means to me."

There was no lightning or thunder, no burning bushes or benevolent voices from the clouds. It struck Maggie as softly as a feather on her brow.

Maggie's voice was gentle but, for once, in command of her emotion. "That's wonderful, Z. Prophets aren't teachers; they're examples. I'm going to follow the example. I'm going to accept life. I'm going home and I'm going to stop the adoption process on this baby I'm carrying inside me. What if I had a Sally and I never knew her?" Maggie stood, leaned forward and gently kissed Zevon's forehead. "Don't let the bastards get you down."

The End